Dear Reader,

How quickly time passes! I can hardly believe we've reached the end of my family saga, The O'Connells. I'm going to miss them. From your notes and e-mails, I know you'll miss them, too, but what better way to say goodbye to these brothers and sisters than to know they've all followed their dreams? That each of them—Keir, Cullen and Sean, Fallon, Megan and now Briana—have found love?

After my last book, the one about Sean, you started asking me about Briana. Said one of you, "Sean needed a special woman, but Briana needs a man who might not even exist." Ah, but he does. His name is Gianni Firelli, and he's one of the most exciting heroes I've ever created. Gianni wants Bree the minute he sees her. She treats him badly, but that doesn't turn him off. And when they're finally alone (but in a rather public place) Bree goes into Gianni's arms and returns his passion with fiery heat. After that, they avoid each other. It's for the best, they think, until a terrible accident robs Bree of her best friend, Gianni of his…and a baby of its parents.

Come with me as Briana O'Connell and Gianni Firelli try to find a way past duty, past passion, and toward deep and abiding love.

I hope you enjoy this final book about the O'Connells. It's hard for me to say goodbye to them, but I'm pleased to have found happiness for them all.

With love,
Sandra

Sandra Marton

THE SICILIAN MARRIAGE

The O'CONNELLS

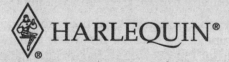

HARLEQUIN®

TORONTO • NEW YORK • LONDON
AMSTERDAM • PARIS • SYDNEY • HAMBURG
STOCKHOLM • ATHENS • TOKYO • MILAN • MADRID
PRAGUE • WARSAW • BUDAPEST • AUCKLAND

ISBN 0-373-12458-9

THE SICILIAN MARRIAGE

First North American Publication 2005.

www.eHarlequin.com

Printed in U.S.A.

CHAPTER ONE

GIANNI FIRELLI was restless.

It was six o'clock on a warm May evening and he'd been trapped at the party celebrating the birth of Stefano Lucchesi's child for what seemed forever.

The room was too crowded, the voices too loud, and if anyone stuck one more squalling baby under his nose, he was going to forget that the expected response to such an affront on a man's eardrums was a smile. Between babies-in-bellies and babies-in-blankets, there were almost enough kids here to field a football team.

It looked as if Stefano had married into a fertile clan.

As if that weren't enough, an hour ago, Tomasso Massini, one of Gianni's oldest friends, had shown up with his wife. His extremely pregnant wife.

You, too, Tommy? Gianni had thought even as he shook his hand, kissed the wife and said all the right things.

The sexy blonde with the endless legs was the only diversion Gianni had seen, but she'd turned out to be as rude as she was easy on the eyes.

Sighing, he cast a surreptitious glance at his watch. Another few minutes and he could make a polite exit. Until then, he'd smile, say the right things, and try to figure out what in God's name had impelled Stefano to give up his freedom and become not just a husband but also a daddy.

Gianni had nothing against marriage or babies. Someday, he supposed, he'd settle down, marry and have a couple of children of his own, but that was way in the future.

Not yet, though. It was much too soon.

Stefano and Tomasso seemed happy enough, but that didn't keep him from puzzling over why two sane men would give up their freedom when they were only in their thirties.

Was it something in the air?

He'd almost said that to Tomasso, but you didn't joke with a man whose wife had a belly the size of a boulder, not even if you'd known him since you were ten. He, Tommy and Stefano had grown up together on the crowded streets of Manhattan's Little Italy. Their paths didn't cross often anymore but they were there for each other when it mattered.

Obviously babies mattered.

Somebody—one of Stefano's new brothers-in-law—brushed past him, a screaming infant in his arms. A smell wafted from the child.

It wasn't baby powder.

"Sorry," the guy said, and grinned.

Gianni managed a smile in return. "No problem," he said, and headed for the terrace where he took a deep, deep breath of fresh air. Okay. He'd stay out here where he could enjoy a little quiet along with the view of Central Park forty stories below and think about whether he wanted to see Lynda tonight without having to pretend he was delighted that his two best friends had obviously lost their minds.

Maybe he should have stayed with his instincts and opted out of this party. He'd been tempted to send a gift from Tiffany's, tuck in a note explaining how sorry he was he couldn't make it in person, etc., etc., etc., but how could he not show up at this celebration for Stefano's child? He'd missed the wedding—bad weather that shut down all the airports had seen to that.

So, he was here.

The blonde with the up-to-her-ears legs was here, too.

Gianni scowled. Was he back to that? Well, there was nothing else to think about. The lady had made an impression. A negative one. And, since he hadn't come up with much else to do after he'd made the rounds, his thoughts naturally returned to her.

He'd had a toothache once. Try as he had, he couldn't keep the tip of his tongue from returning to the offending molar.

This was the same ridiculous thing.

Gianni looked into the Lucchesis' enormous living room. There she was now, talking animatedly with Tomasso's wife, Karen, as if they were old friends. She smiled, she touched Karen's arm, she even grinned.

She hadn't even managed a tilt of the lips for him.

Not that he cared. She wasn't his type at all. He preferred his women petite, dark-haired and quintessentially feminine. Lynda met those standards. She was also all curves, where the blonde was as skinny as a boy. Lynda smiled when a man smiled at her. The blonde didn't. She meted out favors with the stinginess of a miser opening his purse.

A waiter stepped out on the terrace. "Something to drink, sir?"

Gianni nodded, took a glass of red wine from the tray and raised it to his lips.

He and the blonde had arrived in the lobby at the same time. The doors of the private elevator for the penthouse were closing when he heard a voice call out.

"Hey," a woman said.

A slim hand had thrust between the doors.

Gianni hit the button that reversed the doors' direction. They opened, and he saw the blonde.

Not my type, was his first thought.

He gave her a polite smile. "Sorry. I didn't see you coming."

She gave him a long look. Her expression was one of suspicion.

"This is a private elevator," she said.

Gianni's smile tilted. "Indeed it is."

"It only goes to the penthouse."

"How convenient," he said dryly. "That happens to be where I'm going."

"Did the doorman—"

"Perhaps you'd like to see my driver's license, passport and birth certificate," he said, his smile fading. "Or perhaps I should ask to see yours."

That, at least, had put a stain of color across the arcs of her high cheekbones.

"I'm going to the Lucchesi party."

"So am I. Or, at least, I will once you step inside and the doors shut."

She entered the elevator and stood beside him, eyes straight ahead. Okay. He'd decided to give it another try.

"Are you a friend of Fallon's?"

"No," she said, without looking at him.

"Stefano's?"

"No."

"Then are you with—"

"I don't see that it's any of your affair," she said, still staring straight ahead. Then she turned toward him, her eyes cold as ice. "Besides, I'm not interested."

It was his turn to be the one whose face stung with heat.

"I assure you," he said, "I'm not—"

The elevator stopped, the doors opened. Gianni stepped out first without waiting for the woman to precede him. It was a good thing the car opened directly into Stefano's foyer. He wasn't sure what he'd have done if they'd ended up in front of an apartment door and he'd had to decide whether to ring the bell or tell her she could go straight to hell.

Pathetic, he knew. Even more pathetic that she'd reduced him to such childish musings. He'd almost told her what he was thinking but he'd spotted Stefano coming toward him and he'd smiled, only to have the blonde sweep past him, give a little squeal of delight and run straight into Stefano's arms.

"Stefano," she'd cried happily, and Gianni, mouth thinning in disgust, had let himself blend into the crowd.

Apparently the Ice Princess reserved her smile solely for a favored few.

Now, watching her, he saw her flash that smile for Stefano's wife and baby daughter as she took the child from Fallon's arms. He saw her lips purse as if she were cooing. The baby kicked its legs and the blonde not only smiled again, but she threw back her head and laughed.

It was quite a laugh. Husky. Throaty. Under the right circumstances, he suspected that laugh would be sexy as hell.

Gianni narrowed his eyes.

He could see he'd made some errors about the woman. They were unimportant, given the circumstances, but he was a man who liked to get the details straight. Her hair wasn't blond, it was half a dozen shades of palest gold. And she wasn't skinny. Slender, yes, but with rounded hips and a nicely defined backside.

And when, still laughing, she hoisted the baby high in the air, her breasts lifted and only a blind man wouldn't have noticed that they were round and full...

And not confined by a bra.

The pale green silk dress clung to her body just enough so he could see the outline of her nipples.

What were they like? Small? Large? What color would they be? Rosebud-pink, he imagined, like her mouth. Soft to the touch, silken and responsive. They'd tighten under his caress, bloom under the laving of his tongue...

Hell, what was he doing?

This was a christening, not a stag party. And wasn't it a good thing he was on the terrace so he could turn his back to the room, because his wandering thoughts were having an all-too-predictable effect on his anatomy.

Gianni concentrated on the Manhattan skyline, bathed now in the variegated orange hues of the setting sun, but thinking about the colors of things wasn't a good idea right now. It took him straight back to the blonde's breasts.

Green was a better color. The green of the boxwood, growing in some of the terrace's many planters.

The green silk of the woman's dress and the way it molded to her...

"She's beautiful, isn't she?"

Stefano had come up beside him, grinning, holding out a bottle of wine. Gianni nodded and held out his glass for a refill.

"Was it that obvious?" he said with a rueful smile.

"Are you kidding? Of course."

Gianni sighed. "Thanks a lot."

"Hey, I'm only speaking the truth."

"Easy for you to say, Lucchesi."

"Well, sure, but who wouldn't react to such beauty?"

"Let's not go overboard here," Gianni said. "She's attractive, assuming you like the type."

"Attractive?"

"Yes. You know, she's got all the right equipment in all the right places." Stefano was looking at him as if he'd lost his mind. He thought back to how the blonde had greeted his old friend, married or not. "But that doesn't make her gorgeous."

"That's a joke, right?"

"Why would I joke? I'm dead serious. Plus, she's got all the charm of a tarantula."

Stefano's expression turned grim. "You'd better be glad

you and I've been friends since P.S. 26, Firelli, or I'd pin your ears back.''

''What wrong with you, man? You'd take me on because I don't agree a woman's gorgeous?''

''Damned right I would. This particular woman is—this woman is…'' Stefano's eyebrows rose again. ''What woman?''

Was this what happened to a man when he married and had a child? Did he lose his sanity as well as his freedom?

''The blonde, of course,'' Gianni said impatiently. ''The one who greeted you with such, uh, warmth…and, by the way, doesn't Fallon object to that kind of thing?''

Stefano's eyes widened. Then he threw back his head and roared with laughter.

''Wonderful,'' Gianni said coldly. ''I'm glad you think this is—''

''The blonde,'' Stefano gasped. ''Oh my God, the blonde!''

''That's it.'' Gianni slapped his glass on a nearby table and started toward the doors.

Stefano grabbed his arm. ''Where are you going, you idiot?''

''Lucchesi,'' Gianni said through his teeth, ''I'd hate to wipe up the floor with you while your guests watch, but so help me—''

''I was talking about my daughter!''

''Yes. And I told you…'' Gianni blinked. ''Your daughter?'' He felt the color rise in his face. ''You were talking about—about—''

''About Cristina. Of course. And you thought I was talking about a woman.''

''Hell.'' Gianni turned away, leaned his arms on the terrace railing and stared blindly into the gathering dusk. Things were going from bad to worse. ''You're right,'' he mumbled. ''I'm an idiot.''

Stefano chuckled. "I'm happy we agree." The men fell silent for a minute. Then Stefano cleared his throat. "So, which blonde are we talking about?"

"It doesn't matter," Gianni said, waving his hand in dismissal. A couple of seconds went by. "The one who damned near threw herself into your arms when she got here."

"Not a very good description, Firelli. All women throw themselves into my arms."

Gianni chuckled. "Better not let your wife hear you say that."

"Better not let his wife hear what?" Fallon said, smiling as she joined the men. "Gianni, it's good to see you again."

Gianni smiled and kissed her cheek. "And you, Fallon. Motherhood has made you even lovelier. I wouldn't have thought that possible."

Fallon batted her lashes. "You Sicilians! You always know how to make a woman feel good."

"Some women," Stefano said. Fallon raised her eyebrows. "It seems one of our guests turned down the chance to have her name added to Gianni's little black book."

"Stefano," Gianni said warningly.

Stefano slipped his arm around his wife. "Come on, don't be shy. If you're interested in one of our guests—"

"I'm not," Gianni said quickly. "I only said—"

"Point her out," Fallon said. "I'll introduce you."

Gianni looked at Stefano, who was grinning from ear to ear. "Damn it, Lucchesi! Fallon, your husband's letting his imagination run away with him."

"I know who she is," Stefano said, as if Gianni weren't there.

"You don't," Gianni said quickly. How in hell had this gotten away from him so fast? "There must be half a dozen blondes at this party."

"But you said this one threw herself into my arms."

"And?"

"And that she was attractive." Stefano winked at his wife. "Attractive, mind you, but not beautiful."

"What," Gianni said coldly, "is your point?"

"My point," Stefano said smugly, "is that I know who she is." He paused, just long enough so that Fallon and Gianni gave him their full attention. "The lady in question is my sister-in-law."

Gianni stared at his old friend. "Your—"

"He was talking about Briana," Stefano told Fallon. "And why would a man who thinks a woman is attractive but not beautiful be fixated on her?"

"I am not fixated on her. I've never found that type of woman interest… Oh, hell. I'm killing myself here, aren't I?"

"Yes," Fallon said agreeably. She let go of her husband and linked her arm through Gianni's. "And the only way out is to let me introduce you to Bree so you can find just what, exactly, it is you never find interesting."

Stefano and Fallon were laughing, so he laughed, too, or tried to, as she all but dragged him into the crowded room. Thank God, he thought, after a quick look around. Bree or Briana, whatever her name was, was gone.

"I'd love to meet her," he said, lying through his teeth. "Too bad she seems to have left."

"She went upstairs to diaper the baby," Fallon said, heading for the curving staircase that led to the penthouse's upper level, "and I'm not going to let you back out of this."

"Fallon. Look, I'm sorry. I shouldn't have said what I said about your sister. I'm sure she's charming. Beautiful, too. And—"

"Bree," Fallon said, "there you are," and Gianni turned from his hostess and looked at the woman coming down the steps toward them.

He'd gotten it right the first time.

Briana O'Connell wasn't beautiful.

She was spectacular.

All that blond hair, tumbling over her shoulders to frame a face dominated by sea-blue eyes. That mouth, yes, rosebud-pink and just full enough to make him wonder how it would feel to sink into its soft warmth. The high breasts, slender waist, delicately rounded hips and long, hell, endless legs.

At least she wasn't trying to freeze him with a look. How could she, when she gave him a glance that lasted no more than a second?

"Bree, this is Gianni Firelli. Gianni, my baby sister, Bree."

"It's Briana," the blond vision said, and turned her attention to Fallon. "The baby fell asleep as soon as I put her in her bassinet. I left her with her nanny. Is that all right?"

"It's fine. Uh, Bree? Gianni's one of Stefano's oldest friends."

This time, Gianni got the full force of her icy gaze. "How nice for them both. If you'll excuse me…"

"Why should I excuse you?" he said, before he could stop himself. He stepped away from Fallon, moved closer to Briana and pitched his voice slow enough that only she would hear him. "Are you always so rude, or is this personal?"

Those deep blue eyes met his and suddenly he saw something in their depths, a flash of heat so intense it threatened to sear his soul.

"You flatter yourself," she whispered.

And then she was gone.

Gianni had never understood what people meant when they said their blood was boiling, but he understood it now. He stared after her, imagined the pleasure of going after her, grabbing her and shaking her until she begged for mercy…

Or of swinging her into his arms, carrying her away, taking her to a room where he could strip her of that green dress and that icy look, put his hands in her hair and kiss her until she was helpless and pleading for more...

"I'm terribly sorry, Gianni."

He blinked, focused his eyes on Fallon's face. She looked as shocked as he felt.

"Bree's not— She's not a rude person. I don't know what came over her."

Summoning a smile wasn't easy, but he managed. "It's all right."

"No, it's not. Look, let me go find her and—"

"No." His voice was sharp. Carefully he manufactured another smile and started over. "Really, Fallon, I'm not offended."

"Well, you should be. When I get her alone later—"

"Forget it. Maybe she had a difficult day."

"Bree? A difficult day?" Fallon gave a ladylike snort. "I don't know how. My sister doesn't do anything that might be considered difficult."

Except treat men as if they were contemptible, Gianni thought, but he wasn't going to say anything like that. Her sister's behavior wasn't Fallon's responsibility.

"Doesn't she have a job?"

"An endless succession of them. She's been a photographer, a travel consultant, a salesclerk, a game show research assistant..." Fallon smiled. "Our mother says she's still finding herself but to be honest, my other sister and I don't think she ever lost herself in the first place. She's just, well, flighty."

It was a nice way of saying Briana O'Connell was unreliable, not just rude and sullen. The woman wouldn't be any sane man's type, let alone his.

"Fallon," he said, taking his hostess's hands in his, "I've had a wonderful afternoon."

"You're not leaving?"

He smiled and brought her hands to his lips, pressed a light kiss to the back of each.

"I'm afraid I must. I have a dinner appointment this evening."

"Ah. Too bad. Stefano and I hoped you'd stay after the others left. He loves to talk about old times with you."

"Another time, I promise. Make my goodbyes to him, will you?"

"Yes, absolutely." Fallon linked her arm through his as they walked slowly through the foyer. "And Gianni... I'm really terribly sorry about my sister."

"No need. I've been rebuffed before."

Fallon laughed, turned to him and cupped his face in her hands.

"You're a bad liar, Gianni Firelli. We both know that there's not a woman alive who wouldn't do a maidenlike swoon if you smiled in her direction."

"From your lips to God's ear," he said lightly.

She laughed again, rose on her toes and pressed a demure kiss to his lips.

"It was good seeing you. And thank you for the beautiful gift for Cristina."

"My pleasure. *Ciao,* Fallon."

"Goodbye, Gianni."

The elevator was waiting. He stepped inside, kept smiling until the car doors closed. Then he let the scowl he'd been fighting darken his face as he took his cell phone from his pocket.

Lynda answered on the first ring. "Hello," she said in that breathless whisper that always made his muscles tighten.

Strangely enough, they didn't tighten this time.

"It's me."

"Gianni." Her whisper became a purr. "I hoped you'd call. Are you coming over?"

The elevator reached the lobby. He stepped briskly from the car, nodded to the doorman when he opened the door that led to the street.

"Let's have dinner."

"Of course, darling. Are we going out? Shall I put on something pretty... Or shall I stay as I am? I just took a bath and all I'm wearing is that pink silk robe you gave me."

Pink. Rosebud-pink, like Briana O'Connell's mouth.

"Gianni? Can you hear me?"

He cleared his throat. "I hear you, Lynda."

"What do you want to do? We could try that new restaurant everyone's talking about. You know, Green Meadows. It's supposed to be spectacular."

Green, like the dress that outlined Briana's supple body. Spectacular, like her magnificent face...

"Gianni?"

All at once, Gianni knew what he wanted to do. It had nothing to do with Briana O'Connell. Nothing at all. It was just something that had been coming for a few weeks, and it was time he dealt with it.

"Lynda?"

"Yes?"

"Don't bother making reservations. I'll be there in twenty minutes." He paused. "And get dressed," he added gently. "All right?"

He heard the swift intake of her breath. "Gianni? Is everything all right?"

"Twenty minutes," he said, and pressed the disconnect button.

An hour later, he left Lynda's apartment for the last time. She was crying and he hated knowing he'd made that happen but at the very start of their relationship they'd agreed neither of them was interested in commitment, and that when the time came to end things, they'd do it with honesty.

"I know," she'd said tearfully, when he'd reminded her of that, "but I thought things had changed."

Nothing had changed. It never did. Women always said one thing at the start of a relationship and another at its end.

Gianni sighed. Darkness had finally claimed the city and he was eager to get home, take a long shower and put the strange day behind him. He thought of hailing a cab, then decided he'd rather walk.

Tomorrow, he'd send Lynda something to cheer her. A bracelet, perhaps. Something expensive enough to assuage her tears and his guilty conscience because honesty was one thing, but dissolving a relationship with no warning was another.

The truth was, he really hadn't thought about ending things until a little while ago. He'd been satisfied enough until he'd gone to that damned party. Until he'd looked into the eyes of a woman who didn't seem to care that he existed and saw, in those eyes, something else.

That one swift, blinding flash of heat.

A sharp wind blew down 57th Street, surprisingly cold after the warmth of the day. Gianni turned up the collar of his jacket, tucked his hands deep in his pockets and picked up his pace.

CHAPTER TWO

"WHY DIDN'T YOU like him?"

Bree looked up from her salad. There it was, the question she'd been waiting for since Fallon phoned and asked her out to lunch. The only surprise was that it had taken her sister a week to make the call and almost half an hour to ask the question.

"Who?" Bree said innocently. Why give away more than was necessary?

"You know who. Gianni Firelli."

Bree popped a grape tomato into her mouth and chewed contemplatively. She had two choices. She could say "Who?" and pretend not to know what her sister was talking about, or she could tell her to mind her own business. Neither response was going to get her very far. Growing up, she'd learned what that determined tilt of her eldest sister's chin meant.

The best thing was to tackle this head-on.

"I assume," she said, putting down her fork, "we're talking about the fact that I didn't fall at the man's feet."

"Fall at his feet? A simple 'Hello, nice to meet you,' would have done it."

"I said 'hello.'"

"You know what I mean, Bree. You almost took his head off."

"I did not."

"Yes, you did. I can't believe you behaved so badly!"

Behaved so badly? Bree's chin lifted, just like Fallon's. "And *I* can't believe you still think I'm six years old."

"You were rude."

"I was honest."

"Being rude isn't being honest."

"Your opinion, not mine. Are you going to eat that last croissant?"

"No. And don't change the subject."

"I'm not changing anything. I just don't want to be badgered."

"Your manners were appalling."

"I don't know how to break this to you," Bree said sweetly, "but you're my sister, not my mother."

"And a good thing, too. If Ma's plane hadn't landed late, she'd have been at the party in time to see you in action. Can you imagine how she'd have reacted?"

"No." Bree's tone had gone from sugary to saccharine. "Why don't you tell me?"

Obviously Big Sister hadn't expected a reply to what she'd meant as a rhetorical question.

"Well, she'd have—she'd have—"

"Sent me to my room without supper? Docked my allowance?"

The sisters glared at each other. Then Fallon sighed.

"Okay, maybe I'm overreacting."

"Hallelujah," Bree said, picking up her fork again.

"But you really were abrupt."

"I wanted to be sure Mr. Firelli got the message."

"Which was?"

"That I wasn't interested."

"Gianni's a very nice guy."

"No doubt."

"And he's good-looking."

"Good-looking?" Bree shrugged, put down her fork and reached for the butter. "I suppose."

"Give me a break! You know he's good-looking."

"What I know," Bree replied, breaking off a piece of croissant and buttering it, "is that Gianni Firelli is gorgeous."

"Well, of course he is. He's…" Fallon blinked. "What did you say?"

"You heard me. He's, what, six-one? Six-two? Shoulders out to here, solid muscle straight down to his toes, black hair, green eyes, a face like a Greek god's—"

"Italian," Fallon said, staring at her.

"A minor detail. The point is, the man's incredible. An out-and-out hottie." Bree reached for her glass of white wine and smiled at the dumbstruck expression on her sister's face. "Give me a break, Fallon. I'm not dead! Did you think I hadn't noticed?"

"I don't know what I thought," Fallon said, sitting back in the booth. "Tell me more."

"What more is there? I'm sure there were a dozen women at your party who'd have happily killed for the chance to be introduced to him."

"But?"

"But, as I already told Karen—"

"Karen?" Fallon said, bewildered.

"Karen Massini. Tomasso's wife."

"Oh. Right. I keep forgetting you and she knew each other before I married Stefano."

"Only for years and years," Bree said, rolling her eyes. "We were friends in college. Close friends. Then she married Tomasso, moved to California and we lost touch, but ever since she got pregnant and they moved back to New York—"

"Yes, okay, I remember," Fallon said, impatient to return to the current topic. "So, you and Karen talked about Gianni?"

"She said she'd noticed him looking at me and… You know how these things go."

Fallon wanted to reach across the table and shake her sister. *Don't try to play matchmaker, cara,* her husband had told her at breakfast. *Gianni and Briana didn't connect. End of story.* Stefano had taken her in his arms. *Not everyone is lucky enough to fall in love at first sight.*

No. Not in love, perhaps, but something had happened between Stefano's old friend and her baby sister. Fallon was certain. Karen wasn't the only one who'd noticed the way he'd looked at Bree. And the way Bree had looked at him, even as she was giving him the brush-off.

"No," she said carefully, "I don't know how these things go. What did Karen say?"

"Oh, I don't remember, exactly." Bree patted her lips with her napkin and pushed away her plate. "Something about me taking pity on the guy and at least giving him a smile."

"You see? You were so impolite that people noticed. Poor Gianni."

"Poor Gianni," Bree said, the words coated with sarcasm, "needs your sympathy the way a bear needs a fur coat. He has a mistress."

"Oh."

"Yes. Oh. A mistress, and he was coming on to me anyway. What do you think of him now? Or didn't he bother mentioning that we'd met in the elevator and he tried a pickup line before the doors had the chance to shut?"

"Well," Fallon said, thinking back to the first time she and her husband met, "well—"

"Look, there's just something about the guy I don't like, okay? End of story."

"Bree. Honey, you've gone through how many relationships? Sooner or later, there's always something about the guy you don't like, whatever that means. Don't make a face. I know you're a big girl—''

"An adult," Bree said coolly, "but neither you nor Megan seem able to hang on to that thought."

"We just want you to be happy. To find someone to love."

"Lust isn't love."

Fallon blushed. "Sometimes it's the way love begins."

"Well, not for me." Bree's expression turned dreamy. "I'll meet the right man someday. He'll be gentle and sweet. He'll never do anything to upset me. He might not stand out in a crowd, but—"

"What about passion?"

"Sex isn't all it's cracked up to be."

"Passion isn't only about sex," Fallon said softly, "but if you think that making love isn't special, you haven't been with the right man."

"Sex Ed 101," Bree said and, just as she'd hoped, her sister laughed. Good. She really didn't want to get into this topic. "Don't worry about me, okay? And lunch is on me. No arguments."

Fallon watched Briana rummage in her handbag. "Bree?" she said, so softly that Bree looked up. "This passion thing. I know you. You're full of fire. Full of life. Why would you want to deny it?"

"Amazing," Bree replied, trying for a light tone. "Karen made the same speech. Do the two of you really think you know what's best for me?"

"I barely know Karen, but I admire her insight. Did you ever consider we might be right? Maybe you're kidding yourself. Maybe what you really want is a man who'll sweep you off your feet?"

Briana's eyes flashed. Fallon had pushed too far. It was time for the truth.

, "Sweep me off my feet, huh? Like our father did to our

mother?'' She leaned forward, all attempts at good humor gone. ''I was the baby, so maybe you think I don't remember, but I do. Ma struggling to pretend it was okay with her whatever he did, smiling when she wanted to cry, never saying an unkind word to him or about him.''

''Bree—''

''Our mother turned herself into a doormat because of that 'sweeping her off her feet' crap. She lived for our father, lived *through* him, and if you think I'm going to let myself in for the same nonsense, you're crazy!''

''Is that how you think of me?'' Fallon said quietly. ''As a doormat for my husband?''

''No! I didn't mean—''

''Stefano swept me off my feet. Qasim swept Megan off hers, and one look at our sisters-in-law and I could tell it was the same for them. We're all head over heels, passionately in love with our husbands. Are we all doormats?''

''No, no, I never…'' Bree took a steadying breath. ''This is pointless,'' she said. ''I'm just not looking for passion. If it works for you, great, but I know myself. I want—''

''Something quiet.''

''Yes.''

''Something undemanding.''

''There's nothing wrong with that!''

''Something safe,'' Fallon said softly, and reached for Bree's hand. ''What are you afraid of, sis?''

''Nothing,'' Briana said quickly, and even as she said it, she knew she was lying.

She *was* afraid. Of the dreams she'd had about Gianni Firelli each night since the party. Of the way he'd made her feel. Of that one cataclysmic instant when she'd looked into his eyes and felt the earth tilt under her feet.

Of losing herself, her dreams, her hopes, her very being, in the fires of passion.

MAY BECAME JUNE, and June slipped into July.

The days were hot and muggy. New Yorkers who could afford it abandoned the city in droves. You were more likely to bump into your Fifth Avenue neighbor on the beaches in the Hamptons or on village greens in the Connecticut hills than in the city.

Gianni didn't notice the heat. He was immersed in a trial that was finally nearing its conclusion. It had been a complicated case, one that required his personal attention. He'd gone back and forth to the coast several times, even now, in the trial's final hours. Days took on a numbing similarity when you spent them on airplanes.

Invitations came in, as they always did: dinner parties at the beach, long weekends in the country. He hadn't dated anyone since the break-up with Lynda. Word had gotten out and hostesses everywhere were doing their best to inveigle him into meeting eligible women, but he wasn't in the mood. He wasn't in the mood for parties, either. Not since May. Not since Briana O'Connell had treated him with a curtness that had bordered on contempt. He needed closure.

Entering his penthouse on a Friday evening, tired after another round of flights and depositions, Gianni grimaced at that overused word. Closure was the feel-good term of the decade.

In this case, though, it was true.

He shrugged off his jacket, undid his tie and the buttons on his shirt as he made his way to the bedroom.

Lack of closure was why he couldn't get what had happened out of his mind. He was furious with himself that he hadn't told the lady what he thought of her, but how could he? He'd been a guest in Stefano's home, and she was Stefano's sister-in-law.

Gianni tossed his cuff links on the dresser, added his wallet and change, peeled down to his briefs and started for the shower before remembering the heavy vellum envelope the doorman had given him. It had been hand-delivered.

Gianni eyed the envelope narrowly. It was, surely, some kind of invitation. The delivery by messenger, the vellum stock were dead giveaways. Well, whatever he'd been invited to, he wasn't going. He wasn't in the mood for people and small talk but someone, somewhere was waiting for an answer and he believed in being polite even if...

Hell.

He tore open the envelope and felt his bad mood dissolve. Tomasso and Karen had had their baby. A girl. His smile turned into a grin. They were having a Welcome to the World party for the child. Karen's idea, without question. Gianni didn't know her well but from what he'd observed and from what Tomasso said, Karen was the antithesis of her pragmatic husband. She was day to his night, Tomasso had told him with the kind of smile that made it clear it was a winning combination.

Gianni's grin faded. Damn it, the party was tonight.

Sighing, he shut his eyes and rubbed the back of his neck. Lord, he was tired. The last thing he was in the mood for was a party, but another life had come into the world and even if he couldn't yet understand the appeal of fatherhood, he wanted to clap Tomasso on the back, kiss Karen and wish them well.

Gianni dropped the invitation on the dresser and headed for the shower.

Tonight, at least, nobody would try to play matchmaker, not with the baby the center of attention.

Better still, there wasn't a snowball's chance in hell he'd run into Briana O'Connell.

"Hallelujah," he muttered, and stepped under the spray.

So MUCH for snowballs and hell.

He ran into the Ice Princess just minutes after walking

into the party. At least, he would have if he hadn't spotted her and come to a screeching halt.

She was standing with a group of people, her back to him, but that didn't matter. The hair tumbling down her back, the endless legs, showcased by heels so spiked they should have been declared a hazard to a man's health, were dead giveaways.

All her attention was focused on a guy doing his best to make her laugh. Damned if he wasn't succeeding.

Gianni felt his muscles tense. This woman laughed easily for anybody but him.

What was she doing here? Tomasso, he thought grimly, and just then, Tomasso had the misfortune to stroll by. Gianni grabbed his shoulder and glared.

"Did you invite her?"

"Invite who?"

"Damn it, Tomasso… No. You wouldn't do that to me. It was Fallon."

"It was Fallon what?" Tomasso said, his bewilderment so genuine that Gianni knew he was blameless.

"Fallon who put Karen up to this. To inviting Briana O'Connell." Gianni jerked his head in Bree's direction. "Stefano's wife is the only one who'd—"

"Nobody put Karen up to anything. Briana is Karen's best friend."

It was Gianni's turn to look shocked. "Her best friend?"

"Well, they'd been out of touch for a few years, but yeah, best pals, way back when. They went to college together. Roomed together. They were sorority sisters. You know, the whole nine yards." Tomasso raised an eyebrow. "What's the problem?"

"Nothing," Gianni said wearily. "There's no problem."

"You sure?" Tomasso offered a friendly leer. "You and she have something going on?"

"Only if you'd describe a spider as having something

going on with a fly.'' Gianni laughed and slung his arm around the other man's shoulders. "How about taking me to meet that new daughter of yours?''

The baby was cute, as babies went. The food was good, the ale was cold, and twenty minutes after he'd arrived, Gianni was ready to leave.

World War Three had not erupted. The Ice Princess either didn't know he was here or she knew he was here and was ignoring him. She was still chatting with the same group of people. The only thing that had changed was that now he could hear her laugh.

It was the laugh he'd heard at Stefano's. Husky. Sexy. Secretive.

It was driving him out of his mind.

How could she laugh when he was so royally ticked off? How come she didn't know he was here? She had to know. He hadn't been aware of the connection between her and Karen, but she'd certainly known he and Tomasso were friends, and—

And, he didn't have to worry about her driving him insane because he was already climbing the steps of the asylum. Why else would he stand here watching her? Why would he give a damn? Why would he feel his temper rising and his blood pressure increasing?

Okay. All right. Closure. Wasn't that what he'd wanted? He felt a muscle jump in his cheek. Closure was what he'd get, and right now.

There must have been something in his face as he strode across the room because the people she was with fell silent. Only one man was still laughing; a look from him and the laugh turned into something that sounded like a caw.

"What's the matter?'' Briana O'Connell said.

She swung around and he saw the surprise and something more flash across her face, something he would have missed if he weren't feeling it himself.

Desire, hot, raw and savage, sluiced through his blood.

"You," she said, so dramatically that he almost laughed.

"Me," he said, and reached for her arm.

"Hey." She tried to pull away. He wouldn't let her. "What do you think you're doing?"

"Yeah," the man who'd been laughing said, "what do you think you're doing?"

Gianni swung toward him. "Whatever I'm doing," he said pleasantly, "it's none of your business." The guy's face turned a sickly grey. Okay. Maybe he didn't say it pleasantly. "The lady and I have things to discuss."

He looked at Briana. Her face was as pink as the guy's was grey. He could see the pulse beating in her throat. Was she afraid of him? She ought to be. He'd had about all he was going to take.

"You're crazy. We have nothing to—"

She gasped as he slid his hand to her wrist and encircled it.

"Don't give me a hard time."

"You son of a bitch," she said, her voice trembling, but it was there again, swift as the beat of a hummingbird's wing, that flash of heat flaring in her eyes.

Gianni stepped closer.

"Your choice, princess. Are you coming with me, or do I pick you up and carry you?"

"Bree?" the guy said, and Gianni grudgingly gave him credit for having more balls than brains.

She hissed a word he hadn't thought she'd know, then slicked the tip of her tongue across her bottom lip. He felt his body tighten in response. When she tore her hand from his, he let her do it. He knew it was the small victory she needed so she could spin on one of those wicked stiletto heels and head for the front door.

He was no more than a step behind her.

Did somebody call his name? He didn't know, didn't

care, didn't think about anything but the swing of her buttocks, the way her short lemon-yellow skirt flared around her thighs as she strode from the apartment.

The elevator was just outside, waiting for them as if he'd planned it. She stepped into the car and jabbed a button. He stepped inside and she tried to shoot past him just as the door began to close. His vision clouded; he grabbed her arm and spun her toward him as the doors slid shut.

"Let go of me!" She jerked under his hands, eyes hot, breasts rising and falling with each quick breath. "What in hell do you think you're doing?"

"What I should have done the day we met," he said, and he hauled her against him and kissed her.

She cried out, but the sound was lost against his plundering mouth. She beat her fists against his shoulders and tried to twist her face away from his but he tunneled his hands into her hair, angled her face to his, and kissed her again.

"Bastard," she panted, "you no good bas—"

And then she wound her arms around his neck and opened her mouth to his.

The first taste of her and he was lost. She fell back against the wall of the car, her body arching against his, breasts soft against his chest, hips lifting to the thrust of his.

"Oh God," she whispered. "Oh please…"

Gianni groaned, cupped her backside and lifted her. She wrapped her legs around him, pressed herself against his erection and he felt a rush of desire so primitive it was almost his undoing.

"Tell me," he said. "Say it. Say you want me. That you want this."

"Yes. Yes!"

He slid his hand under her skirt. Only a scrap of lace lay between his questing fingers and her flesh. She was hot and wet and when he felt her against his palm, he had to fight for control all over again.

He stroked her, then slid a finger inside the damp fabric that kept him from her, and she cried out, dug her fingers into his hair, kissed him with the same urgency he felt, the same blind need.

And the car rocked to a stop.

The doors opened. They must have, because the next thing he knew, he heard a startled gasp, a laugh, saw Briana's eyes open, heard her horrified cry.

Gianni didn't turn around. He reached out blindly to the control panel and hit a button. The doors shut. The elevator began to descend again.

"Briana," he said, "Bree..."

She twisted against him with the desperation of a wild creature caught in a trap and struck out with her fist. He grunted when one blow connected with his jaw.

"Damn it," he said, grabbing her hands as she slid down his body, "will you listen to me?"

The elevator reached the lobby. She shot from the car as if the demons of hell were at her heels. The surprised door-man yanked the front door wide with only seconds to spare, then stared at Gianni.

"Sir? Is everything all right?"

Gianni drew a ragged breath as he stepped from the car.

"Everything's fine," he said, and knew it was the biggest lie he'd ever told in his life.

CHAPTER THREE

AUGUST in New York always was hot, humid and altogether unbearable. The last thing any sane human being would do in such weather was stand over an ironing board, especially when the AC was gasping its death throes, but that was what Bree was doing early on the first Monday of the month.

Ironing was mindless. You could listen to the radio, hum along with an Elton John oldie and let your thoughts drift on the calm seas of boredom. That was what Bree was doing.

For instance, right now, she was thinking about whether or not to go to her brother's beach house on Nantucket Island. Cullen and Marissa had invited her up for the weekend.

"The weather's gorgeous," Marissa said when she called, "and we're going to have a barbecue. Nothing fancy. We'll just invite in some interesting neighbors."

Bree sighed as she spread a silk blouse over the ironing board. "Some interesting neighbors," in female-speak, was sure to mean "some interesting men." Her sisters and sisters-in-law, still basking in the glow of their own happiness, kept trying to fix her up with the right man. She'd already met a handsome vintner, thanks to Cassie; a suave hotelier, courtesy of Savannah; a sexy sheikh, compliments of Megan, a hotshot CEO, pointed in her direction by Fallon, and now Marissa wanted to introduce her to a Nantucket something-or-other.

One thing was certain. The O'Connell women all had

impeccable taste. The men they'd set in her path were handsome, charming and, she was sure, great catches.

It wasn't their fault that not a one was as gorgeous, as sexy, as altogether spectacular as Gianni Firelli...and, she was certain, not a one of them was the same kind of rotten SOB.

Bree brought the iron down with enough force to smooth out a wrinkle in a sheet of steel.

She'd tried to forget about him. Forget that elevator ride. Forget that she hated herself for not having dealt with him properly. Now, here he was, back in her head.

It was the heat. The damned heat. Bad enough it was a million degrees outside and almost that in her apartment. Was this a day to sweat over a hot iron in her tiny kitchen?

It was, if you were going on a job interview.

Too much heat and humidity could turn your brain to mush. She couldn't afford that. She had a job interview in less than an hour. Why waste time thinking about something that was history?

Yes, she'd behaved like an idiot. Yes, the memory still made her cringe. Yes, she wished she'd slapped Gianni Firelli's face but—

But, she hadn't.

The interview. She'd think about the interview. About how difficult it was to get the miserable wrinkles out of this miserable blouse because the iron was too hot and the ironing board table didn't stand straight on the worn linoleum floor. The stupid legs wobbled...

Her legs had wobbled, when Gianni kissed her.

The faint scent of scorched silk rose from the ironing board. Bree snatched the iron off the blouse. Too late. There was a brown spot right on the collar the size of a quarter.

"Damn, damn, damn!"

Washable silk, the tag said. Light pressing might be required. Light? An elephant could sit on the blouse for an hour and the wrinkles would still be there as soon as it lifted its butt. And what difference did it make? Five minutes on the street, she'd look as if she'd slept in it, anyway.

Truth was, she'd probably look that way as soon as she put it on. She was sweating. Not glowing, the way those la-de-da fashion magazines said. Sweating, with a capital S.

No wonder the rent was so cheap. Well, cheap for New York City. When she'd signed the lease a few months back, she'd figured she was getting a bargain. Some bargain, she thought, as she shoved her hair back from her face.

The kitchen faucet leaked. Only one of the stove's burners worked, and there wasn't any point in talking about the air conditioner. It was supposed to cool the whole place—not much to ask, considering the size of this shoe box the landlord called an apartment.

Pitiful.

And so was she.

Bree yanked out the plug and stood the iron on its heel. That was the only way to describe a woman who was fixated on something that was weeks in the past. A man came on to you like a savage, forced his kisses on you...

Another time, another place, a woman who'd endured such indignities would have gone straight to her brothers and asked them to defend her honor. She wouldn't do that, of course—this was the twenty-first century, not the middle ages, and besides, she could handle her own affairs—but the thought of the male contingent of the O'Connell clan beating Gianni Firelli to a pulp held definite appeal.

Never mind that she'd seemed to respond to what he'd done. If she had, it was only because he'd taken her by surprise. Okay. So she hadn't handled the scene well. So what? Why keep thinking about it?

Why keep thinking about the taste of his mouth, the feel of his hand between her thighs?

Bree said a word that would have stunned her protective

brothers, crumpled the blouse into a ball and hurled it across the room.

As if she gave a pig's whistle about any of that.

The job interview. She had to concentrate on that. She needed to be at her best, look her best and how was she going to manage that with Mr. Firelli in her head and a scorch mark the size of Texas on her blouse?

The blouse was easier to handle.

She could stand the collar up. Or wear a scarf around her neck. No. The collar wasn't made to stand up. As for the scarf—Fallon would probably make a scarf look like an ascot.

She'd make it look like a noose.

Bree dumped the blouse on the bed. What to wear? She needed this job. She didn't know anything about being a gofer for a TV producer but she'd learn. She had to. What little she'd saved from her last stint as a waitress was about gone, and an hour spent yesterday with the Sunday *Times* employment section had been depressing.

The city seemed in desperate need of everything from accountants to zoologists. Unfortunately two years of college didn't qualify her for much of anything.

"You and me, kid," Sean used to say. "All the O'Connells are busy being grown-ups, except us."

Bree stepped into the shower and turned the water cold enough to raise goose bumps.

That wasn't true anymore. Sean, the untamable gambler, had been tamed. He'd sunk his winnings into ownership of an exclusive Caribbean resort while she still drifted from job to job and place to place, searching for something she'd like enough to want to do for the rest of her life.

The score, thus far, was a big, fat zero.

She shut off the shower, stepped onto the mat and wrapped herself in a bath sheet.

Who'd want to make a career demonstrating cosmetics to

bored matrons with more money than common sense? Spend a lifetime selling *prêt à porter* to spoiled rich girls? She'd have been one of those overindulged brats herself if it weren't for the fact that she flat-out refused to accept help from her family.

Financial help, anyway, and when she'd tried the other kind...well, it hadn't worked out. Waiting tables at Keir's vineyard restaurant last winter had gone well enough until she'd not-so-accidentally dumped a glass of wine on a pain-in-the-ass customer who'd complained about everything from the first course to the last.

More recently, Fallon had wangled her a stint modeling for a new diet drink photo shoot.

You probably weren't supposed to stab your index finger between your lips and make gagging noises when the guy watching from the sidelines was the client's rep. Even so, he'd hit on her. That had been even more nauseating. He was okay to look at, she supposed, but nothing compared to...

Bree frowned into the mirror. "Stop that," she said out loud, and marched to her closet.

What did TV people wear, anyway? Was the desired look funky or professional? Maybe a little of each. The navy silk suit, but with that *Bella Sicilia* T-shirt she'd picked up last time she visited Fallon and Stefano.

The doorbell rang.

Bree rolled her eyes. What now? The super had already come by to peer at her air conditioner and tell her there was nothing he could do until a new part arrived. Her usual early-morning visitor, Mrs. Schilling from across the hall, had already stopped by to update her on the alien spaceship on the roof.

Brring, brring, brring.

Time for another bulletin on the Alien Invasion.

Bree sighed, knotted the bath sheet more tightly over her

breasts and went to the door. She undid the hundred and one locks—each brother had added his own assortment—and cracked the door a couple of inches.

"Yes, Mrs. Schilling," she said, "have you heard something more from the Mart—"

The words caught in her throat. It wasn't her slightly-batty-but-sweet neighbor standing on the doormat, it was her impossibly arrogant would-be seducer, the man she'd spent the last few weeks loathing. Here he was. In the flesh. The gorgeous flesh.

What had taken him so long?

"You!" Oh God, such originality! And such a stupid thought. Bree stood straighter. "What are you doing here, Firelli?"

"I have to see you."

He wasn't much on originality, either...and why should such a hackneyed phrase make her pulse beat zoom? Definitely, the heat was frying her brain.

"A charming line," she said brightly, "but wasted on me. I am absolutely not interested in—"

"Briana. This is important. Let me in."

Like the big, bad wolf, he made the simple words sound tempting. That was the bad news. The good news was that she wasn't some silly little creature in a nursery rhyme.

"Not in a million years."

"We have to talk."

"We have nothing to talk about. And if, by some miracle we did, have you ever heard of that new invention called the telephone?"

"Damn it, this isn't a game. Let me in."

"You're right. It isn't a game." Bree started to close the door. "Go on home, Firelli. Give us both a break and just—"

"Briana." Gianni moved forward and wedged his shoulder in the narrow opening between the door and the jamb. "Please."

The word, as much as that shoulder, stopped her cold. Please? She wouldn't have thought the term was in his vocabulary. At least, not when it came to women. She started to tell him what he could do with his plea but something in his eyes made her reconsider.

"Something's wrong," she said slowly.

He didn't answer. "Open the door, Bree."

"What is it?" A coldness began stealing over her. "Gianni? What's the matter?"

"I've come to tell you something," he said quietly, "but not like this. Let me in."

Her heart gave an unsteady thump. "Tell me what's going on."

Gianni ran his hand through his hair. It was already standing up in little curls, as if he'd repeated the same action several times. Now she noticed he was wearing jeans, a T-shirt and running shoes, and there was a shadowy bristle on his jaw.

Gianni Firelli, unshaven and casually dressed at this hour on a weekday morning?

"Stefano," she whispered. "And my sister…"

Her knees buckled. Gianni cursed and caught her by the shoulders.

"No," he said sharply. "Listen to me, Bree. Your sister and brother-in-law are fine. Your family is fine. This has nothing to do with them."

"Then what… It's something bad, isn't it?"

She was staring at him, her eyes enormous in her suddenly pale face, and the anger he'd been riding since the last time he saw her drained away. He had bad news for her. Terrible news, the worst imaginable.

He had to tell her that her best friend was dead.

Gianni drew a long breath. "Bree—"

"Briana? Is it the Martians?"

He looked over his shoulder. An old woman was standing in the doorway opposite, hands clutched to her breasts.

"Have the aliens demanded our surrender?"

Any other time, he would have laughed. The woman was staring at him as if he were the devil himself, which pretty much described how he felt at the moment.

"I'm a friend of Briana's," he said gently. "Everything's fine."

The old woman looked uncertain. "Are you sure?"

"The president says we'll never surrender," he said firmly, and forced a smile to his lips.

That seemed to do it. She stepped back inside her apartment; Gianni moved forward, still holding Briana by the shoulders, and kicked the door shut.

Heat and humidity curled around him like the breath of a swamp. The room reminded him of a closet. He felt too big for it and for the emotions churning in his belly.

"Tell me," Bree said.

"Sit down first."

He knew the second she figured it out. What little color had returned to her face drained away.

"It's Karen," she whispered.

Gianni swung her into his arms. Two steps, and he was beside a tattered sofa. Carefully he lowered her to it. She scooted into the corner, watching him as if he held the secrets of the universe.

"Please. Tell me what happened. It *is* Karen, isn't it?"

A muscle tightened in Gianni's cheek. "Yes."

Tears flooded her eyes. "Oh God," she said brokenly. "Oh God!"

"And Tomasso," he said, rushing the words, knowing she had to hear it all and hear it quickly before the sledgehammer blow of pain struck him again.

"Both of them?"

"Yes."

Her head fell back, as if she'd been hit. Gianni moved closer and clasped her hands.

"I'm sorry, Briana."

"It can't be." She made a choked sound that was almost a laugh and was, he knew, the first sign of hysteria. "It isn't possible."

"I'm afraid it is."

"But how? How could—"

"They were in Sicily, visiting Tomasso's grandmother. They were driving. The roads there are narrow. Twisting. Another car—the driver was drunk. He—he—" Gianni couldn't get the words out. His throat felt as if someone were gripping it, trying to choke the air from his lungs. "It was quick," he finally said. "They didn't suffer."

Bree's eyes had become dull. Suddenly they flashed to life. "The baby?"

He nodded. At least there was some good news. "The baby is fine."

Briana began to weep, silently at first, then in great, gasping sobs that tore at his heart.

"*Cara,*" he said thickly, and drew her into his arms.

She cried uncontrollably. He felt his eyes grow damp. He wanted to weep with her but he hadn't cried since he was five and he'd realized that if he did, his father would only beat him harder.

Instead he buried his face in her hair as he tried to figure out how to tell her the next part. Surely it would seem as impossible to her as it had to him when Tomasso's attorney phoned early this morning, first with the brutal news of Tommy's and Karen's deaths, and then with the details of their will.

"Are you sure?" he'd kept asking the man, which was incredibly stupid because he was a lawyer, too; he knew the Massini attorney couldn't have misunderstood. But the other man was patient. He read the pertinent clauses aloud. Even after that, Gianni kept saying, *yes, but are you sure?* because what he was hearing couldn't be right.

"Give me your fax number," the exasperated attorney finally said. Minutes later, Gianni had been staring at a document that would change his life.

His, and Briana's.

"When?" Bree said.

Her tears had stopped but she was still in his arms, her face hidden in the crook of his neck.

"Two days ago. Their lawyer called me this morning."

"Two days ago."

Bree shuddered against him. The room was hot, almost airless, but she was probably in shock. And she was wearing nothing but a towel.

A towel.

Gradually he became aware of the feel of her against him. The softness of her skin. The warmth of her breath. The silky strands of damp hair, tickling his nose.

"Bree."

He clasped her shoulders, tried to ease her from him, but she shook her head and burrowed closer.

"Bree," he said again, and stroked her back. Her skin was as silken as her hair, and bore the fragrance of flowers.

She was an oasis of life in a sea of death.

He understood that. Still, he despised himself as he felt his body beginning to quicken.

"Karen was my best friend," she whispered.

"As Tomasso was mine."

"We met in college, but it was as if we'd always known each other."

"Yeah." He cleared his throat. "Tommy and I were friends since we were ten."

"I just—I can't believe—"

"Neither can I."

She gave a soft sob that tore at his heart. He drew her closer and began to rock her in his arms.

"To think of them both gone…"

"Shh," he murmured, pressing a kiss to her hair. They sat in silence for a few minutes and then Briana looked up at him.

"What about—what about the funeral?"

"It's over," he said gruffly. "Tommy's grandmother made the arrangements. She's an old woman. I don't think it occurred to her that Tomasso and Karen had friends in the States who'd want to attend."

"So we—we can't even say a proper goodbye."

The pragmatist in him wanted to tell her that the Massinis wouldn't know the difference but the pain he felt, the pain he knew she felt, made him offer a different answer.

"They knew we loved them," he said quietly. "Perhaps they know it still."

Briana began to weep again. Gianni whispered to her, stroked her cheek, her hair, and suddenly she tilted her face up to his. Her eyes were enormous, as bright as stars; her mouth trembled.

"At least they had each other."

"Yes. They were lucky."

"It's terrible, to be alone."

"Terrible," he whispered back, and he would never know which of them moved first, he or Briana, but a heartbeat later his mouth was drinking from hers, her arms were wound tightly around his neck, and his mind was emptied of everything but her taste, her scent, the soft reality of her in his embrace.

He lay her back on the couch and kissed her throat, felt the leap of her pulse against his lips. Her hands were in his hair; her sighs were sweet affirmations of the power of life.

"Bree…"

She drew his head down and silenced him with another

kiss. Her lips were soft; her body was warm and alive under his hands and when she moved against him, whispered his name, Gianni was lost.

With a groan, he tore open the knotted towel. Her breasts were beautiful, rounded and small with delicate nipples the color of roses.

"How lovely you are," he whispered.

"Touch me, Gianni. Please. Please…"

Her breasts. They fit his palms as if they'd been fashioned to do exactly that. She whimpered with pleasure as he cupped them. He bent his head to her and sucked first one beaded tip and then the other into his mouth.

She sobbed his name, raised her hips in age-old invitation, asking a wordless question that could only have one answer and he gave it, spreading the towel fully so he could see all of her: the narrow waist, the rounded hips, the golden triangle between her legs.

He kissed her there, seeking the perfect pink bud nestled between her thighs with the tip of his tongue. She tasted sweeter than honey and when she arched toward him and cried out her passion, the blood roared in his ears.

"Gianni," she sobbed, "Gianni, please, please, please…"

"Yes," he said hoarsely, and in a single, swift movement he unzipped his jeans, came down to her, lifted her to him and entered her, sinking deep, deeper than he ever had before, and then she tightened around him and he stopped thinking of anything but this, this, this…

Her wild cry of fulfillment triggered his own release.

For an instant, for an eternity, the world hung suspended.

And then it was over.

Gianni's body sang while his brain recoiled at what he'd done. He rolled away, searching for the right words. Briana scrambled up against the back of the sofa, grabbed for the towel and clutched it to her.

"Oh God," she said brokenly. "Oh God…"

"Briana. I'm sorry. I didn't mean—"

"Don't say anything. Just—just go away."

Her mane of golden hair was a wild tangle that obscured her features. He wanted to pull her into his arms, smooth it back, lift her face to his and tell her he hadn't meant to take her like this, that what had happened in the elevator wasn't what he'd wanted, either.

What he wanted was to make slow, tender love with her. To kiss her mouth, then trail kisses down her throat to the hollow between her breasts until she was trembling with desire. He wanted to enter her slowly, watch her face as he did, take her with him to the heavens and hold her close as she came back to earth.

But she was glaring at him, disgust and hatred bright in her eyes. He knew that reaching for her would be a mistake. Hell, everything he'd done since they'd met had turned out to be a mistake.

"Damn it, are you deaf? Get out!"

She sounded as if he were a monster who'd attacked her. Gianni felt the first stirrings of an emotion far safer than regret.

"Look," he said carefully, "these things happen."

"These things?" she said, and the coldness in her voice was the final touch he needed.

"Sex," he said bluntly. "It's an affirmation of life. It's what people often turn to, in the face of death."

He was right. Briana knew that. She'd read books, seen films; she wasn't stupid. People had sex for reasons that had nothing to do with desire.

And that was the worst of it. That she'd done this for all the wrong reasons. Dreamed of being with this man, ugly as that was to admit, dreamed of it since the night in that elevator, and now that it had happened, it had nothing to do with Gianni wanting her or her wanting him; it had to do with the loss of someone who'd been like another sister.

"Briana."

She looked up. Gianni's tone was cool. He sounded like a man about to make a speech instead of a man who'd just— who'd just—

"We have to talk."

"You're wrong, Firelli. We don't have a thing in the world to talk about."

Slowly he rose to his feet. Color flooded her face as he zipped up his jeans. He didn't even have the decency to turn away.

"Forgive me," he said in a voice that implied anything but regret. "For a minute there, I thought the Ice Princess had been replaced by a woman."

"I'd rather be made of ice than be a savage like you."

He reached out so quickly that she didn't have time to get away from him, grasped her by the arms and hauled her to her feet.

"Be careful, *cara,* or do you want me to remind you of just how easily I can turn you from cold to hot?"

"Get—out!"

"Believe me, I'd love to. But—"

"But what? Damn it, leave right now or I swear, I'll have you thrown out!"

A muscle jumped in his jaw. Slowly he lifted his hands from her and took a step back.

"Tomasso and Karen left a will."

"So? I can't imagine what that has to do with me."

"Apparently Karen disagreed with my assessment of you."

"What are you talking about?"

"She must have thought you had a heart." He paused, and she saw the muscle in his jaw flicker again. "She and Tommy named you guardian of their baby."

She blinked. "What?"

"They named you Lucia's guardian."

"That's impossible. Karen would have said—"

"Impossible or not, it's a fact."

Briana sank down on the couch. "But I'm not—I mean, I don't know anything about—"

"Perhaps they understood that." He folded his arms over his chest and even managed a thin smile. "You see, they didn't leave the entire job to you."

"I don't—I don't understand."

Gianni took a deep breath. "They named us both as guardians. You. And me. We're going to raise this child together."

CHAPTER FOUR

BREE STARED at Gianni. What he'd told her was impossible...but people didn't joke about death, and funerals, and certainly not about the guardianship of helpless children.

A mistake, then. Yes, of course. A mistake. She said that to Gianni. He shook his head.

"Unfortunately it isn't." He took a sheet of folded paper from his back pocket. "See for yourself."

Bree looked at the paper. She didn't want to take it from him. Maybe if she didn't, it wouldn't be real. Gianni gave her no choice. He shook it in front of her face like a matador dancing his cape before a bull.

"Read it," he said impatiently. "Then tell me if you still think it's a mistake."

It was a fax transmission, dated only a few hours ago. She clutched it with both hands and did what he'd asked, but the words made no sense. At first, she thought it was because she was still in shock from what Gianni had told her. Then she realized it was in Italian.

"I don't—it's in Italian."

Hell. Of course it was in Italian. Gianni cursed himself for being a fool, grabbed the fax and translated it in rapid English. Bree heard a numbing string of legalese, whereases and wherefores and whomsoevers tumbling after each other like drops of rain.

Evidently lawyers in Europe couldn't manage a simple sentence without enough fifty-dollar words to render it almost indecipherable any more than their counterparts in the U.S.A.

Not that it mattered.

The only important words were those that confirmed what Gianni had already told her. Karen and Tomasso had designated them as joint guardians of their baby.

"...so charging Briana Claire O'Connell and Gianni Fabrizio Firelli with the responsibility to raise our daughter, Lucia Vittoria Massini, to make all decisions for her as they see fit, until she reaches the age of majority."

Gianni looked up. Normally he hated legal jargon. Not this time. Reading the will in the impersonal language with which it had been written made him feel more comfortable.

Perhaps he could handle this better if he donned the cloak of the law.

"Questions?" he said briskly.

"The age of...?"

"Majority. The point at which a child ceases to be a minor."

"I know that," Briana said sharply. "I meant, what age is that in Italy?"

"Eighteen."

"And here?"

"The same."

"I thought girls married younger in the old country."

"They marry when they marry, and what in hell does that have to do with anything?"

"I was just thinking—you know, not about when Lucia will marry but when she'd be considered old enough to marry. Or vote. Or..." Gianni's eyebrows were aiming for the ceiling. Who could blame him? Bree waved her hand and sighed. "I guess I was trying to figure out when she'll stop being a minor."

"When we're too old to give a damn," Gianni said, stuffing the fax back in his pocket.

To his surprise, Bree laughed.

"You find this amusing?"

"No. No, of course not. It's just the way you said that…"

"Well, it's true." He sank down on the sofa next to her. "The child is only three months old."

"Four."

"Oh, well, that's a big improvement. We only have seventeen years and eight months to go."

Bree's lips twitched. Gianni glared at her and then his did, too.

"My God," he said softly. "Pity the poor kid. You and me, parents?"

"Guardians," she said quickly.

"Parents, guardians, what the hell's the difference?" His smile faded. "Listen to us, wondering how such a thing could have happened when all that really matters is that Tommy and Karen are gone." He turned toward Briana. Her smile faded, too; her blue eyes were filling with tears. "Bree. About—about what happened before…"

"Don't."

"I want you to know that I never meant to… When I took you in my arms, I only meant to comfort you."

"Yes. I know."

"I had no intention of taking advantage of you. Of the situation. It's just that—that the news about the Massinis—"

"You don't have to explain, Gianni. I understand why—why we did what we did."

Gianni nodded. "Good." He reached for her hand. "Because we're going to have to get along from now on."

"We'll get along just fine," Bree said stiffly, tugging her hand free of his, "as long as we forget about what happened."

Forget that they'd made love? That he'd heard her cry out his name as she tumbled off the edge of the world?

"Of course," he said politely.

She nodded. "Good. Because if this is going to work, you have to promise me that we'll forget this—this incident."

"I understand."

"I'm going to get dressed. Then we can decide how best to handle the situation."

Gianni smiled pleasantly. "Fine."

She walked away, head high, like a queen in full regalia instead of a woman in a towel. He had to give the lady credit. She had guts.

But he deserved some credit, too. He was getting really good at telling lies where she was concerned, first a couple of months back, when she'd run from him and he'd assured the doorman that everything was fine and now again, when he'd assured her he'd forget they'd made love.

He wouldn't forget. He was damned sure she wouldn't, either.

Not with him around to remind her.

BREE KEPT IT together until she was safely inside the bedroom but once she'd shut the door, she began to shake. Sitting down on the edge of the bed was like sitting on a raft in the middle of the ocean.

The mattress felt as if it were tilting. The room spun. She'd never fainted in her life but she didn't need a medical encyclopedia to tell her she was close to it now.

And she couldn't let that happen. If Gianni heard a thud, he'd be here in a heartbeat. The last thing she wanted was to let him see how much the entire morning had shocked her.

Or to let him see her all but naked again. God, no. Never.

What was that meditation thing she'd tried back in college? Take a deep breath. Hold it. Now blow it out. And again. Just a couple more…

The mattress stilled. The room stopped spinning, and the world went from black and white to color. Bree bowed her head. Was she losing her sanity, or was the world going crazy? A little while ago, the problem of the day had been getting a job. Now it was figuring out what it meant to be the guardian of a helpless infant...

What it meant that she'd let a man she despised make love to her.

A tremor shuddered through her. "Be honest," she whispered. She hadn't "let" Gianni make love to her, she'd begged him to do it. He was the one who'd held back; she'd initiated the kiss, all but offered herself to his caresses.

And "making love" was the wrong way to describe what had happened. They'd come together the same as they had in the elevator. Hungry. Eager. A fusion of mouths and bodies...

"Briana?"

Bree jerked her head up. She could hear Gianni's footsteps stop outside the door. Her heart leaped. Had he come for her? Was he going to take her in his arms again?

"Bree?" Transfixed, she stared at the door, waiting for the knob to turn.

"I'm going to make some coffee. Okay?"

He was asking her permission to make coffee? She bit back the swift rush of hysterical laughter struggling to surface.

"It's fine," she called. "The coffee's in the cupboard over the—"

"I already found it."

So much for asking permission. She waited until his footsteps faded away. Then she threw aside the towel and jumped into the shower again, scrubbed fiercely with a loofah though she suspected not all the scrubbing in the world would wash away the scent of Gianni's skin, the feel of his hands...

Oh, the feel of his hands…

"Stop it," she muttered, and turned her face up to the spray.

Five minutes later, dressed in the blue suit, a white blouse and sensible heels, her hair yanked back in a lòw ponytail, she walked briskly into the kitchen. Gianni was leaning against the counter with a mug of coffee in his hand. Another mug sat beside the coffeepot. He reached for it but she shook her head.

"I'll pour my own, thank you."

One dark eyebrow rose but he didn't say anything. A good thing, too, she thought grimly as she sipped at the hot coffee. News of the tragedy had stunned her; being named guardian had been a second shock but the shower had cleared her head. She was ready to deal with things now.

As for what had happened with Gianni—just as she'd told him, there was no point thinking about it. It was over.

What they had to do now was work out a way to supervise the baby's life, and to arrange things so that she and Gianni spent as little time as possible with each other.

She knew exactly how to accomplish that.

"All right," Gianni said, and cleared his throat. "Here's what I've been thinking…"

Bree held up her hand. "I have an appointment."

Both of his eyebrows went up this time. "Excuse me?"

"An appointment." She glanced at her watch. "Actually I *had* an appointment, but I'm going to head on uptown anyway and see if—"

"Let me get this straight. I've just told you that we have a child to raise, and you have something to do that's more important than talking about exactly how we're going to do it?"

Bree's eyes flashed. "I have a job interview to go to. A job, Firelli. You know what that is, don't you? Something people do to earn their living instead of sitting back and collecting fees from fat-cat clients.''

Gianni cocked his head. ''You have me all figured out.''

''Unfortunately for you.'' She checked the time again. ''I'll meet you at six this evening. There's a coffee shop on—''

''Is that what your brother does?''

She looked at him. ''I beg your pardon?''

''Cullen. He's a lawyer, isn't he? Does he sit back and collect fees from fat-cat clients?''

Why on earth had she said that? The truth was, she didn't even know what kind of law Gianni practiced.

''Because I don't, you know.'' He drank some coffee. ''Collect fees from fat-cats.''

''Actually I don't much care who you—''

''I'm with the Attorney General's office. I'm a federal prosecutor.''

She blinked. ''In three thousand dollar suits?''

Gianni made a deliberate show of looking down at his jeans and T-shirt.

''I don't mean now, I mean—''

''I know what you mean,'' he said, very softly. ''And I'm glad to see you haven't forgotten our last meeting, either.''

''I simply meant,'' she said, hating the rush of heat she felt rising to her face, hating even more the stupidity of the conversation she'd initiated, ''prosecutors must be doing very well these days.''

He gave a negligent shrug. ''I enjoy what I do. I don't make money at it.''

Bree fluttered her lashes. ''Ah. Another member of the silver spoon brigade.''

''Like you?'' he said, not missing a beat, enjoying the new color that was turning her lovely face pink.

He resisted the urge to say ''gotcha.'' He knew little about Briana O'Connell but looking around her cramped apartment, it was easy to see she didn't depend on a dole from her wealthy family.

It was also easy to see that she was doing everything she could to make it clear she didn't like him, including tarring him with a brush laden with stuff he didn't deserve.

He was damned if he was going to let her do it.

"Here's the bottom line," he said. "I have a lot of money, yes, but I earned every penny. I was a litigator for several years." He grinned. "Shearing those fat cats, if you'll pardon the mixed metaphor. I invested wisely, took a surprised look at my bank book one day, said what the hell and went into a field that's more satisfying." He took a last sip of the rapidly cooling coffee. "Anything else you're interested in knowing?"

"I'm not—"

"Of course you are." He turned, put down his cup and tucked his hands into his back pockets. "And I don't blame you, considering that we're going to be spending the next eighteen years together."

He'd meant it as a joke, more to see that magical rush of color to her face and maybe, just maybe, to see that icy *hauteur* slip as she turned from ice princess to a creature of fire and heat again.

But she didn't react as he'd expected. Okay. As he'd hoped. Instead she looked as if he'd just admitted he had the unfortunate habit of turning into a werewolf at the first hint of a full moon.

"I beg your pardon?"

"Eighteen years," he said calmly. Why stop now, when he was already into it? "Minus those four months, of course. Come on, princess. You remember that age of majority we talked about."

"But we won't be spending them together."

"Not entirely, no. Even real parents get a couple of weeks off every now and then."

Her jaw dropped. "What are you talking about?"

What, indeed? He'd come here with his head full of ways they could exercise the terms of Tomasso's will while maintaining distance from each other. Now he wondered how he could have thought of doing that. It would be the wrong way to honor the memory of Tommy and Karen, and completely unfair to Lucia.

Surely there was no other reason for the change in plans he was considering.

"We can discuss it later."

Bree dumped her purse on the counter and folded her arms. "We can discuss it now."

"I thought you said you had a job interview."

"I did. Hours ago. I don't think there's much point in going now." Her tone softened. "Besides, after this about—about Karen…"

"Yeah." He cleared his throat as the reality of what had brought him here hit home all over again. "I know."

"So, let's take things one step at a time. Where's the baby now? With her great-grandmother in Sicily?"

Gianni nodded. "Yes."

"She must be distraught. I mean, after what happened…"

"I agree. The lawyer said the sooner we get the baby, the better."

Bree stared at Gianni. "Get her?"

"Well, we're not going to leave her with Grandma."

"No. Of course not. It's just that…" Bree swallowed dryly. It was hard enough to think of herself as guardian for a child she barely knew but, until now, the discussion had been more or less academic. Now they were getting down to basics. "It's just that the details seem—they seem—"

"Tell me about it," Gianni said gruffly. "You know anything about kids?"

Bree thought about her newly found status as aunt. She

could change a diaper and give a bottle. Did that mean she knew about kids?

"No," she said honestly. "Do you?"

Gianni laughed. "Do I look like a man who knows about kids?"

"The happy bachelor," she said coolly. "Running from the altar as fast as his feet can carry him."

"I don't see you with a noose around your neck, either, O'Connell."

"Is that how you see marriage?"

"It's how I see long-term relationships," he said bluntly. "Someday, yeah, I suppose I'll want to have a family…"

"No need to explain. I feel that way, too. I'm not ready to settle down."

"So I gather."

"What's that supposed to mean?"

Gianni shrugged. "Stefano says you're a butterfly, flitting from place to place."

"Stefano talks too much." Bree peeled off her suit jacket. The kitchen felt like a sauna and seemed smaller than it already was. Gianni, lounging casually against the wall, damned near dominated it. She thought about continuing their conversation in the living room, but right now she wasn't sure she'd ever be able to look at the couch without blushing. "Could we talk about this somewhere else?" she said abruptly. "There's a coffee shop downstairs."

Gianni glanced at his watch and shook his head. "I'm late for a deposition. We'll meet later. Seven, at *Luna's*. Do you know it?"

"On 57th just off Madison, but—"

"We'll have a drink, then some dinner, and talk. How's that sound?"

Like a date, Bree thought. Did he think what had happened earlier would happen again?

"I can't make it," she said politely. "We can meet at five, at the coffee shop."

"You have a date?"

He said it casually, as if it meant nothing to him. So much for his thinking of tonight as a date. Now that she thought about it, why would he? What had happened this morning meant no more to him than it did to her. She'd been weak, that was all, letting a moment of grief be eased by a moment of passion. If it had seemed special it was only because of her heightened emotions. It wasn't him. Wasn't his touch, his mouth, his body...

"Briana? Do you have a date?"

She let out a suddenly shaky breath. "Yes," she said, with a polite smile. "I do."

"Break it."

His voice was soft. For a second, she thought she'd misunderstood.

"I beg your pardon?"

"I said, break your date."

His words had an edge to them now. Oh, yes. This was the Gianni Firelli she knew. Arrogant. Demanding. So full of himself he couldn't imagine a woman saying "no," and what she'd done with him this morning had only helped convince him he was right.

Time to set him straight, Bree thought, and flashed another polite smile.

"No."

His eyes narrowed. That muscle flickered in his jaw again. Slowly, deliberately, his eyes never leaving hers, he straightened and stepped away from the counter.

"Who are you seeing?"

Frasier, in reruns, but she'd never admit that. "It's none of your business."

"Wrong answer, *cara.*"

He was coming toward her, his steps slow, his expression

unreadable. Danger crackled in the air between them like heat lightning.

Bree's instinct was to turn and run but she'd grown up in desert country with mountains just on the horizon. Survival Rule One: if you suddenly found yourself confronted by a mountain lion, you didn't flee. You stood still and faced it.

Showing fear to a predator only fueled its hunger.

She held her ground until Gianni was a hand span away. Then, though she hated herself for showing weakness, she stumbled back two steps.

"You have no right—"

"We have a responsibility now, or have you decided you don't want to accept it?"

"I never said—"

"We need to make plans."

"I know that. I only meant..." Bree bit her lip. How easily he'd put her on the defensive! "Meeting at five instead of seven hardly suggests I'm unwilling to accept my responsibility."

"Our responsibility."

"For heaven's sake," she snapped, "will you stop the word games? Karen wanted me to be one of her baby's guardians, and—"

"We're co-guardians."

"More word games."

"More facts." Gianni reached out and caught one of her curls. He wound it around his finger and tugged lightly so that she had no choice but to close the distance between them. "We share Lucia's custody."

"Fine. At five this evening, we can start drawing up a plan."

"What do you know about plans?" he said, gently rubbing the soft silk of her hair between the tips of his fingers.

"Stefano says you're a gypsy. That you never stay with one thing long enough to put down roots."

"First I was a butterfly, now I'm a gypsy." Bree slapped at Gianni's hand. "Let go, please."

"Why?" He brought the strand of hair to his mouth. "I like the way your hair feels against my lips."

"Stop it. Just—just stop it, right—"

"I liked the feel of it against me when we made love."

Her heartbeat stumbled. Where was a good earthquake when you needed one? She wanted the floor to open and swallow her.

"We didn't make love. We had sex."

Gianni gave a soft laugh. "Now who's playing word games?"

"You know exactly what I mean, Firelli."

"Yes." His arms went around her and he drew her against him. She was stiff, unyielding, but the telltale race of her pulse in the hollow of her throat and the flush rising over her skin told him she was as aroused by being in his arms as he was to have her there. "In fact, I do." He bent his head, brushed his mouth gently over hers. "Next time will be different."

"There won't be a next time."

"No?"

"No."

He gave another of those soft, sexy, oh-so-self-confident laughs while she tried, unsuccessfully, to step out of his embrace.

"Eighteen years is a long time, O'Connell."

"Eighteen…?"

"Uh-huh. That's how long we're going to be involved with each other."

"We won't be involved with each other at all," Bree said with determination. She put her hands against Gianni's chest and pushed. This time, he let her go. "Sharing the responsibility for how Lucia is raised means exactly that."

Gianni folded his arms. "Exactly what?"

"You know," she said, because she wasn't about to admit that she didn't. "We'll meet periodically. Plan things."

"Things?" he repeated in a way that made her want to slug him.

"Things. Schools. Where she goes on vacation." She threw out her arms. "Things."

"Ah."

Gianni rubbed his index finger over the bridge of his nose. Briana followed the gesture. Had his nose been broken sometime in the past? A straight Roman profile, was how Fallon had described it and she'd agreed, but there was the faintest little indentation…

"…in her crib."

She blinked. "I—I'm sorry. I didn't hear what you said."

"I said, I'm sure little Lucia will be happy to hear all about schooling and holidays in her crib." His tone was so sarcastic that Bree could almost see his tongue firmly tucked in his cheek. "She's an infant, Briana. It'll be years before we have to decide on schools. We have to make some immediate decisions about her life."

He was right. Why hadn't she realized that?

"For instance, just off the top of my head, we'll need a baby nurse."

"Yes. Yes, of course we will."

Gianni nodded. "Furniture. Clothes." He gave a delicate shudder. "Diapers."

"Formula. Toys."

"All of that. But the first thing is bringing her home." Gianni paced into the living room with Bree following after him. "There's no room for a baby here," he said, looking around him.

"No," Bree said weakly, "there isn't." Things were hapening too quickly. Of course, she'd be the baby's guardian. Co-guardian. But why would Gianni even think of the baby being here, with her? Was she ready for such a change in her life?

He swung around and faced her, hands on his hips, his eyebrows darkly angled slashes over his eyes.

"Besides, it wouldn't be fair to place all the day-by-day responsibility with you."

"Yes. I mean, I was thinking that, but I don't see how—"

"The apartment next to mine is for sale. The people selling it are even including the furnishings. I'll make the necessary arrangements. With luck, you can move in early next week."

"Now, wait just a minute…"

"It's seven rooms, I think. Maybe eight. I'll get hold of a contractor, have him work out a way to join the two flats."

"Join them? Damn it, listen to me!"

"And you're right about tonight. There's no need for us to meet."

Score one for the home team, Bree thought, staring at him as he paced back and forth while he planned her life, for the next eighteen years of it.

"We can discuss everything else on the plane."

"What plane?"

"The one I'm going to charter."

Well, naturally. He could afford to charter a plane, and he lived in an apartment you could fit in a flea's navel with room left over.

"We can be in Sicily by morning." He swung toward her. "You have a passport, don't you?"

"Gianni," she said carefully, "I am not moving into an apartment adjoining yours. I am not getting on a plane and flying to—"

"You said you were looking for a job."

Her head was spinning. What was happening to her life?

"Yes, but—"

"Well, now you have one. You'll handle the day-to-da
custody details. I'll be there every evening, of course, an
I'll hire a nurse to help you, but... What is it?" he sai
impatiently.

"You cannot just walk in here and—and take over m
life, Firelli. Did it even occur to you to ask if I want to d
this? Move out of my apartment? Live next door to you
Take care of a baby?"

He stared at her for a long moment. She waited for sar
casm or anger but he didn't show either. All he did was no
his head.

"You're right," he said quietly. "I should have asked.'

"Well. Thank you. I'll have to revise my opinion of yo
as an arrogant, self-centered—"

"So I'm asking, Briana. Do you intend to honor ou
friends' dying request or not?"

Briana stiffened as she looked into his suddenly flat eye:
"That's cruel. You're trying to reduce this to one issue bu
it's a lot more complex than that."

"Answer the question, please. Will you do what Kare
and Tomasso wished, and stay and see this through?"

God, how she wanted to hit him! "I told you, it isn't the
simple!"

Gianni grasped her shoulders and lifted her to her toe
"No speeches, damn it! Answer the question. Will you d
it or not?"

She could feel the hate inside her, coiled like a venomou
snake. Hate for him, for how he was taking control of he

"Yes," she hissed. "You know I'll do it. But I'll ha
every minute I'm forced to spend in your company. Ju
remember—"

His mouth came down on hers, hard and hot and de
manding. Bree tried to twist away but he clasped her fac
tunneled his hands into her hair, held her while he took wha

he wanted until, at last, she gave a little cry and parted her lips to his.

His kiss softened, became a low-burning flame that she knew could become a blazing fire in a heartbeat. Stop, she told herself, stop, but that fire was what she wanted. How could she deny it, with his mouth on hers? Bree rose to Gianni, drank him in, lost herself in his kiss.

When he finally lifted his head, she was trembling.

"I'll be back at seven," he said. "Be ready for me."

Then, damn him to hell, he turned on his heel and swaggered out the door.

CHAPTER FIVE

BREE SPENT A WHILE fuming but it didn't last long.

She hated to admit it, but Gianni was right. Lucia was what mattered. Nothing else. She had no choice. Of course she'd be the baby's guardian. She'd loved Karen. Karen wanted her to raise her daughter.

How could she possibly turn away from that?

She just wished Karen had discussed this with her, she thought as she yanked clothing from her closet and tossed it into the suitcase on her bed. Of course she'd have said yes, but then the responsibility wouldn't have come as such a shock. Surely asking someone to raise your child was one of the most important things parents could do. Shouldn't Karen have mentioned it? Shouldn't Tomasso?

Maybe not. The Massinis were young. Life stretched ahead of them. Accidents happened to other people.

Bree dug a wadded-up tissue from her pocket, dabbed at her eyes and determinedly blew her nose.

Now that she thought about it, maybe Karen had intended to tell her she wanted her to be Lucia's guardian. They'd chatted on the phone just a couple of weeks ago. *Tommy and I are planning a trip,* Karen had told her. *Let's have lunch when we get back, okay? You and I haven't had the chance for a good, long talk in ages.*

For all she knew, the baby's guardianship would have been the subject of that talk.

Bree plucked a dress from its hanger, folded it and added it to the things in the suitcase.

Not that it mattered now. Karen and her husband were gone, and she was their baby's guardian. She, and Gianni. Whose idea had that been? Karen's? Tomasso's? Just thinking about that little scene before he'd left enraged her. Him standing there, cool as a cucumber, laying out the life he'd planned for her as if he owned her.

She'd tried telling herself that he couldn't be all bad if Karen had named him as co-guardian but that logic didn't help.

Maybe Tomasso had insisted. *He's my oldest friend,* he might have said. *I want him named along with Briana.*

No. Bree sighed and sank down on the bed next to her suitcase. Karen wouldn't have given in to pressure any more than Tomasso would have entrusted his beloved daughter to someone just because he was an old pal. Gianni was an attorney. Maybe they'd named him not just because he was Tomasso's oldest friend but because of his knowledge of the law.

So, why had they named her? What could they have seen in her? Karen and she were close, and Karen had no family to turn to, but how could she have chosen Bree to raise her little girl when she knew Bree's faults so well?

They'd roomed together at college, met for lunches and dinners ever since. Karen knew, maybe better than anyone, that Bree had yet to find what she wanted to do with her life. Karen knew she was irresponsible, bouncing from job to job and city to city. She knew Bree had never committed to anything.

Or to anyone.

Was that someone you'd pick to be your daughter's guardian? Unless...

A couple of months ago, she and Karen had gone to a lecture together. Actually it was ballyhooed as a Life Energy Event. Bree smiled, closed her eyes and drifted back to the afternoon and Karen's phone call.

"Did you ever hear of James LaRue?" she'd asked.

Bree had laughed. "The only people who've never heard of James LaRue are living on an icefloe in the Arctic."

"Well, Tommy's all set to baby-sit and I have two tickets to LaRue's sold-out, razzle-dazzle, opening night performance at Madison Square Garden. Wanna go?"

As a columnist for a Greenwich Village newspaper, Karen got tickets to lots of things.

"I don't know if I can sit through an hour of motivational mumbo-jumbo," Bree answered, and Karen laughed.

"Two hours," she'd said gaily, "but if it's really awful, we'll leave. Come on. It'll be fun."

So they'd gone. And "fun" didn't even come close. The right word, they'd decided ten minutes into LaRue's act, was bizarre.

What's your Life Energy Score? the guru shouted at his audience.

Five, the audience members yelled back. Or eight or three or any number between one and ten.

"It's ten if you have things like a career goal, if you're dedicated to a cause, if you're in a serious relationship, stuff like that," Karen explained, leaning close and raising her voice so Bree could hear her over the enthusiastic roar of the crowd.

Bree rolled her eyes and asked what happened if your answer was minus four? They grinned at that but when LaRue solemnly announced he was going to come into the audience so people could share their Life Energy stories with him, Karen rolled her eyes, mouthed "Enough," and pointed at the exit.

Talking, giggling, they'd ended up at a hole in the wall joint in Little Italy for pizza and *vino.* Bree, licking cheese off her fingertips, swore it was the best pizza she'd ever had.

"Tommy found it," Karen said. "It's just one of the

bonuses a good little girl from Iowa gets when she marries a Sicilian.''

Bree had laughed. So had Karen. Then, suddenly, she'd reached for Bree's hand and squeezed it.

"Oh, Bree," she'd said softly, "I'm so happy."

Bree had smiled. "Who could have guessed?"

"You know how we used to say we couldn't understand wanting to share your life with a man?"

"Wanting to let him take it over, you mean," Bree had answered, her smile fading. "Are you telling me you've changed your mind? That you think letting that happen is a good thing?"

"I'm telling you that we were wrong. Tommy and I share our lives. It's what I want for you, honey. It's what you deserve."

Bree had thought of a dozen answers, but how could you give any of them to your best friend when she'd all but admitted she'd given up her independence and truly believed doing it had made her happy?

Instead she'd gone for the light approach.

"Aha," she'd said, "I get it. You figure if I get into a committed relationship, I'll stop getting minuses from LaRue the Guru."

She'd laughed. Karen hadn't.

"If they gave points for kindness, generosity and goodness of heart," she'd said fervently, "you'd score a perfect 10."

Briana rose to her feet and pushed down the lid of her suitcase. Was that the night Karen had decided on her? Were her supposed traits—kindness, generosity and goodness of heart—the things she'd looked for when she'd entrusted Lucia to her care?

The suitcase lid fell into place and she shut the lock with a snap.

The only thing she could do now was hope that those

qualities were all she'd need to assume her new responsibility—and make certain that the imperious Mr. Firelli understood that they were in this as equals.

If he thought he was in charge, he was in for a very big surprise.

AT SEVEN, the surprise turned out to be Briana's.

Gianni had said that was when he'd pick her up.

"Be ready for me," he'd said, an overbearing statement with just enough sexual overtone to have put her senses on alert. When the doorbell rang, she was primed for anything...

Anything but the middle-aged man in neatly pressed khakis and pale blue shirt who greeted her with a polite smile.

"Evening, Miss O'Connell. I'm Charles. Mr. Firelli's driver."

Why be surprised? Gianni would have a driver and a big, expensive car to match. Charles took her suitcase and she followed him downstairs to a big, expensive Mercedes.

It made her smile.

"Has something amused you?" Gianni asked as she got into the back seat.

"Nothing," she said, and folded her hands in her lap.

He was so terribly predictable. The car. The way he was dressed—gone were the jeans and T-shirt. He was dressed like a banker in a pale grey suit, white shirt and dark red tie. Even the portable computer, open in his lap, suited the picture of a wealthy, important man doing his best to appear wealthy and important.

He was also gorgeous enough to make her mouth water, but what did that have to do with anything?

"I'm glad to see you're prompt."

Gorgeous, and as egotistical as a Caesar. She wasn't foolish enough to take the remark as a compliment.

"Meaning, you thought I wouldn't be."

"It's too soon to know what I think. Despite what has happened, we don't know each other very well."

The words were as frank as they were true, delivered with all the emotion of a man commenting on the weather, but she thought she saw something flicker in that distant gaze of his that made her skin heat.

"I don't intend to discuss this morning."

"I was referring to our conversation."

He hadn't been. She was sure of it, just as she was sure he was trying to rile her. What could she say in reply that wouldn't sound defensive? She wouldn't rise to the bait.

"So was I," she said coolly. "We got off on the wrong foot. We're in this thing together, like it or not, and we'll need to set some conditions."

"For instance."

"For instance, from now on, you're not going to make decisions without consulting me."

His brows rose. "Have I done that?"

"We're flying to Sicily tonight, in your chartered plane. When we get back, I'm moving into an apartment you've selected. I'm going to care for Lucia with the help of a nurse you'll hire." Bree bared her teeth in a smile. "Have I left anything out?"

To her surprise, Gianni laughed. "Not that I can think of."

"Well, it has to stop. I don't like being told what to do."

"Because?"

He asked the question so politely that at first she thought he was serious. Damn, he *was* serious. *Karen, how could you have done this to me?*

"Because I can think for myself, Firelli, hard as it may be to believe."

"Most of my relationships have been with women who like to be taken care of," he said bluntly.

"Well, I don't need to be taken care of," Bree said coldly. "And this isn't a relationship, not the way you mean. We hold a joint responsibility together. That means we make decisions together."

"I don't like decisions made by committee. It's one of the reasons I didn't join a large legal firm."

"I didn't ask what you liked, I told you how it's going to be. We're in this together, like it or not. We're going to have to make whatever adjustments it takes to make this arrangement succeed."

Gianni closed his computer, folded his arms and gave Briana a hard look. She, like him, had dressed for the seriousness of the occasion: white suit, hosiery, white shoes the kind he'd heard women refer to as sling-back sandals. She looked responsible, reliable—and good enough to eat. Like a vanilla ice cream, one he'd start licking at the top and slowly work his way down, down, down…

Damn it!

He'd spent the afternoon telling himself what happened this morning had gotten his desire for her out of his system.

What a hell of a lie. If anything, he wanted her more than ever.

He knew her taste. Her scent. The little sounds she made when he caressed her. He knew the shape of her breasts, the softness of her thighs…and he was turning himself on just imagining what it would be like to take her again, slowly this time, slowly enough to savor each moment as he brought her to the edge, as she trembled beneath him.

"Did you hear what I said?"

She was looking at him with defiance etched into her face all but daring him to argue. He supposed she was right. They'd have to work together as equals if this arrangement had a chance of working out, but what he'd told her was true. He liked taking the commanding position in a relationship; the women he'd been involved with were content with it, too. He knew it was an old-fashioned concept but it suited him to play the more assertive role. He'd been born in Sicily and raised in an American neighborhood that had its roots deep in the soil of an ancient culture.

His eyes narrowed as he remembered Briana in his arms a few hours ago. She hadn't demanded equality then; she'd been eager to let him master her. To lead her in a dance as old, as powerful, as time.

He could make her bend to him again. He had only to reach for her, pull her into his arms. She'd protest but when he kissed her she'd moan, wind her arms around him, open her mouth to the thrust of his tongue...

Gianni cleared his throat and forced the images from his mind. The child. Tomasso's daughter. That was all that mattered.

"I heard you," he said calmly. "And you're right." The shock in her eyes almost made him laugh. "I shouldn't have made decisions without consulting you."

"No. No, you shouldn't."

"So, which of the arrangements would you like to change?" He cocked his head and took pleasure in watching her struggle to regain the high ground. She had courage. Courage, and beauty enough to stagger a man. It was an interesting combination.

"Perhaps you'd prefer to wait a few days to go to Sicily?"

"Of course not. I only meant—"

"Or maybe you'd rather we flew a commercial jet."

"Don't be ridiculous! You know I wasn't referring to—"

"Is it our new living arrangements that distress you? Would you rather I took an apartment in your building?"

Bree snorted. Gianni looked interested. "Something else you've found amusing?"

"You? Living where I live? That would never happen."

"And the reason is...?"

"It's old, it's dirty, it's cramped. The street is noisy and not particularly safe…"

She blushed. He offered a thin smile. "Sounds like the perfect place to raise a child, doesn't it?"

"All right. You've made your point. But—"

"But, in the future, we should discuss our options when we make decisions that affect us." Us? *Us?* What kind of word was that? "Decisions we make that affect Lucia. That's one of the advantages of living in adjoining apartments. We can talk about things in the morning, over breakfast. Or at night, over dinner…"

He broke off in mid-sentence. What in hell was he talking about? She was thinking the same thing; he could see it in her face. He was painting a picture of domesticity, and domesticity had nothing to do with this. Theirs was a legal arrangement, nothing more. They'd live near each other for expediency but that was hardly the same as living together.

"Let me clarify that," he said. "We'll agree on, let's say, one morning meeting and one evening meeting a week so we can talk over problems, make plans, whatever. How does that sound?"

As if he were making decisions again. Still, the idea made sense.

"Fine."

Gianni nodded. "When we get back to New York, I'll phone an agency about a baby nurse."

"A nanny."

"Right. I'll interview several candidates, narrow the field down to two, and you can… What?"

"*I'll* phone an agency," she said. "*I'll* interview several candidates. *I'll* narrow the field down to two, and then you can interview them and choose one."

Bree waited for his reaction. So much for the idea of shared responsibility. His eyes had grown dark; she figured an explosion was likely, which was why she was stunned when he drew a deep breath, then exhaled.

"All right."

Oh, but he wasn't happy. She could tell by the way he snapped open his computer and glared at it, by the way he never spoke another word except for telling her to fasten her seat belt after they'd boarded the plane.

Five hours later, they touched down at Palermo. He got behind the wheel of a shining black Ferrari that had been waiting at the terminal; she got in beside him.

No driver, she was thinking, when he turned to her and spoke for the first time in all those hours, issuing the same order as the one he'd issued on the plane.

She let him get as far as the word "Fasten."

"Amazing as it may seem," she said sweetly, "I do not need a man to tell me when to buckle my seat belt."

"What you mean is," he said, "you don't need a man for anything."

"Now you've got the—"

She gave a startled cry as he pulled her into his arms and crushed her mouth under his. She struggled but he was relentless, lost in her honeyed taste, in the feel of her. She bit him; he ignored the swift, sharp pain, went on kissing her until she moaned and wound her arms around his neck, just as he'd let himself imagine, her hands in his hair, her body arched against his so that their heartbeats became one.

Letting go of her was the hardest thing he'd ever done. She fell back in her seat, eyes wide with shock. He wanted to tell her he was as stunned as she was, that whatever was happening here was beyond his comprehension, too, but instinct warned him that the best thing he could do right now was say nothing that didn't have to be said.

"Buckle that damned belt," he growled, and gunned the engine to life.

Tomasso, he thought as they sped away, *Tomasso, old friend, what the hell have you gotten me into?*

CHAPTER SIX

RAIN PUDDLES DOTTED the slick coastal road that led toward the Madonie Mountains. A low fog rose from the dark pavement and was pierced by the Ferrari's headlights.

Briana stared straight ahead, her hands tightly folded in her lap.

Gianni hadn't spoken since he'd kissed her, then growled his last order. She'd been too angry to say a word. Angry at him for kissing her, angry at herself for ultimately kissing him back.

And for remembering what it had been like to lie in his arms this morning.

Making love with him had been damned near accidental. Making love? What they'd done had been too quick, too frenzied, too wild to be called that, but oh, it had been incredible. Her skin still tingled where Gianni had touched it. Her mouth still felt the heat of his kisses. She could still hear her own little cries, his groan when he'd thrown back his head and come deep inside her.

She stole a surreptitious glance at the man beside her. He was driving too fast, taking the curves hard, jamming his foot to the floor on the straight-aways, but she'd be damned if she'd ask him to slow down. He'd interpret it as a sign of weakness and she couldn't afford to let that happen. He'd run roughshod over her too many times as it was, especially with that last kiss. Kissing her, forcing her to accept his kiss, was some kind of perversely macho exercise of power…

Forget it. She wasn't going there again.

Bree lay her head back against the seat.

What could Karen and Tomasso have been thinking, to put two such different people into a situation like this?

Not that she gave a damn what Gianni was feeling, but he had to be as upset as she was. Like her, he had to be looking ahead and seeing how impossible this arrangement was going to be. Being a guardian to a baby, having your co-guardian living next door, could only be a nightmare for both of them.

She'd cramp his style.

He'd cramp hers.

Suppose she wanted to bring a man home some night? She could see herself slipping the key in the lock, shutting the door after the man as he laughed softly and tucked her into the curve of his arm. She'd turn her face up for a kiss...

A kiss that would be nothing like Gianni's. It wouldn't be mind-numbing. Dominating. Powerful enough to turn her bones to liquid.

No. But it would be pleasant enough.

And that's all that would happen. A kiss, maybe two. What more would she do, knowing Gianni was right next door? That he might have a woman with him.

Stop it, she told herself fiercely, just stop it!

X-rated images weren't her style. For God's sake, being a mother wasn't her style, either. From waiting tables to motherhood or the next best thing to it, in the blink of an eye. It sounded like the title of a bad autobiography, but that was exactly what had happened to her.

She could learn to handle that, but she wasn't about to let Gianni create a plan for her life that would put him in her face, watching everything she did, telling her what to do and when to do it.

No way.

Headlights appeared in the darkness. A truck whooshed

past. Bree's hair, already tangled by the breeze, blew into her face and she swept it back behind her ears.

He was right about some things. Her apartment, for instance. Truth was, she wouldn't want to raise a child there but it was a quantum leap from admitting that to agreeing to live under his thumb.

Karen and Tomasso must have had some overall idea of how they'd want Lucia raised. It made sense that they'd wanted her to handle their little girl's day-to-day life while Gianni dealt with the legal and financial issues.

She and he didn't have to live under the same roof to accomplish that.

She'd move, but she'd choose where. Nobody was going to make that decision for her, and she'd tell him that when they reached their destination, which had to be soon.

What was the name of that town where they were supposed to make the turn-off?

"Cefalù."

Bree swung toward Gianni. Had she spoken aloud?

"We just passed a sign that said Cefalù but I didn't see how far it is. Did you?"

How could she read a sign when she was trying to figure out what had happened to her life?

"It's night," Bree said sharply. "You're driving like a madman. If you want me to read signs, slow down."

"I like driving fast."

Even in the shielding darkness, she could see the purposeful angle of his jaw and that little muscle ticking just above it, a dead giveaway that he was angry. What did he have to be angry about? She was the one on the losing end of this relationship.

"'I like driving fast,'" she mimicked. "Such a mature response."

"I know this road. I've driven it before."

She looked at him again. "You didn't tell me you'd met Tomasso's grandmother. What's she like?"

"I haven't met her but from what Tommy said, her spine is made of cast-iron and she has ice-water in her veins."

"But he loved her. Otherwise, why would he have come all this distance to let her see the baby?"

"Duty. Honor. Idiocy." Gianni shrugged. "The rules of *la famiglia* run deep in Italian families. Tommy didn't like the woman. He just wanted to do the right thing."

"The right thing," Bree said softly. "And now, he and Karen—"

"They're gone. What matters is their daughter. It's up to me to honor their wishes."

"You mean, it's up to us," Bree said coldly. She shifted in her seat, folded her arms and stared straight ahead. "How quickly you forget that the will said Gianni Firelli *and* Briana O'Connell."

"All right. It's up to us."

The truth was, he suspected Tomasso's grandmother wasn't going to see things that way. He had the feeling he was going to have to do some fancy maneuvering in the next couple of hours. He knew enough about Sicily, Sicilians and their sometimes outmoded codes of honor to be wary, but why tell that to Bree now?

He checked his mirrors, pulled into the next lane and raced past the car ahead of them.

"Tommy's lawyer warned me that *Signora* Massini may try to stop us."

"Stop us from what? From taking the baby? Why didn't you tell me?"

"There's nothing to tell you until we see if that's the case." He checked his mirrors again and moved into the right lane. "I did some research on our situation this afternoon." He glanced at the clock. "Yesterday afternoon," he said with a little laugh. "Hell, I can't remember the last time I slept."

Neither could Bree, but she didn't care about that now.

"And?" she said impatiently. "You did some research, and what? Don't tell me that this old woman Tommy hated is going to demand she raise his daughter!"

Gianni glanced at Bree. Her hair was tangled by the wind and she raised her hands to it and pushed it away from her face, eyes glittering in a way that told him she wasn't going to tolerate an answer she thought wrong.

So much passion. So much emotion. Things were simpler when you lived by the law but he had to admit, there was something about the way this woman embraced life that fascinated him.

There was no middle ground with her, no holding back.

There'd been no holding back this morning, when she'd begged him to take her. When she'd opened her mouth to his kisses, opened her thighs to his touch, wrapped those long legs around his waist...

His hands tightened on the steering wheel.

Forget that. They were involved enough, thanks to the terms of Tomasso's will. Eighteen years of dealing with each other stretched ahead of them. Eighteen years? He knew of marriages that didn't last that long! The only way to survive the relationship was to keep it impersonal. No connections, except as they affected Lucia.

Briana had her life. He had his—but only a fool would try and pretend things wouldn't change. How would he bring women home, with Briana a thin wall away? Not that he brought women home often...

Okay. Not that he ever brought them home. It was easier to spend the night at a woman's apartment. That way, he could get up and leave. After the proper length of time, of course.

Did Briana bring home her lovers? Was that what she

figured on doing, once they were living next door to each other? Gianni's jaw tightened. It wouldn't happen. No men. Not in her bed. No men, period. No affairs. No—

"What's the matter with you, Firelli?"

He blinked, looked at Bree, let out his breath. "Sorry. I was, uh, I was thinking about—about Tommy's grandmother."

"Well, so am I. That's why I just asked if she can break the terms of the will."

"Legally? No. No, she can't."

"Well, then—"

"But if she can find a way to delay things, she might."

"And? What do we do then?"

"We come up with something to convince her she'll be fighting a losing battle."

"Such as?"

"I won't know," he said honestly, "until if and when she makes a move."

Bree sank back in her seat. "And all this time," she said, half to herself, "I've been picturing this wizened little old lady, wearing black from head to toe, sitting outside a cottage on a cobblestone road in a two thousand year old village, just waiting for us to arrive."

Gianni grinned. "You've seen one *Godfather* movie too many, *cara,* though I admit, parts of *la Sicilia* meet that description."

"Not the part I've seen. Stefano's castle," she added, when Gianni looked at her. "Have you been there?"

"I've seen photos." He checked his mirrors again, pulled into the next lane and passed a slower-moving vehicle. "I don't expect the Massini place to be a castle but I think you can give up the idea of it being a simple cottage in a little village."

"Only in *The Godfather,* huh?"

"In real life, too, depending on where you're born, and

whether you're rich or poor. My great-grandfather came from a village not far from here. It's why I know this road.''

"You still have family here?"

He shook his head. "No. But I've been back a few times. I wanted to see where I came from.''

"And?"

"And," he said, giving her a quick smile, "the town that might have been the setting for a couple of those movies.''

"Should I be addressing you as Don Firelli?" Bree said lightly.

"If my great-grandfather had had his way, you'd probably be doing exactly that," Gianni said, with no trace of humor. "We're coming up on another sign. I'll slow down. See if you can read it this time.''

He eased his foot off the accelerator. Bree all but pressed her nose to the glass. The sign still flashed past—he must have dropped all the way to eighty or ninety miles an hour, she thought, rolling her eyes—but she was able to decipher it.

"It says we're twenty kilometers from Cefalù.''

"Good. There should be one more sign for the town before we reach our turn-off. Keep your eyes peeled.''

"Were you serious about your grandfather?"

"Great-grandfather. Very serious.''

"He was in the Mafia?"

"He was a *bandito*. There's some question whether he was also *Mafioso*.'' He grinned. "But he was a man of high moral principle. At least, that's the family lore.''

No wonder Gianni had such an imperious attitude. It was in his DNA.

"We just passed another sign. Was it for Cefalù?"

Was it? She hadn't noticed. She was too caught up in imagining Gianni as a bandit. Gorgeous. A little dangerous. Sexy.

She sat up straight. "You're going too fast again," she

said irritably. Who cared if he was descended from *banditos,* gorgeous or not? "How can I read anything, especially in a language I don't speak?"

"You don't have to speak Italian to read a sign." He glanced at the speedometer. "And I'm not going too fast."

"I'm sure that'll be a great comfort to Karen's little girl if we end up as roadkill."

Gianni shot her a narrow-eyed look. The lady had a way with a phrase.

Still, she was right. The Ferrari was a thoroughbred, begging to run, but the baby, their responsibility to her, was all that mattered. He let a few seconds pass to show Briana who was boss. Then he eased his foot off the accelerator.

"You're right. Lucia's welfare is what's important." He glanced at her. "What do you know about babies?"

"Not much."

"But you're—"

"A woman?"

Gianni almost laughed at the dangerous edge in her voice. "You're an aunt. That puts you one-up on me."

Bree sighed and sat back in her seat. "You can put what I know in a thimble and have room left over. Babies cry. They smile. They eat. They sleep. Mostly, they pee and poop. Why Mr. Firelli, sir, was that a shudder?"

"We'll need things."

"Things?"

"A crib."

"A car seat."

"A car seat," Gianni said, and craned his neck to look into the almost non-existent rear compartment of the Ferrari.

"There are laws back home about car seats, but I was thinking about the flight. I can hold her while we drive to Palermo, if you promise to drive slowly—assuming you even know how to drive slowly—but we should buy a car seat to put her in on the plane."

"Of course," Gianni said.

What he meant was, what in hell was happening to his life? Bree knew that because she was thinking the same thing.

"I suppose," he said, "we should discuss how to deal with Tomasso's grandmother."

"Discuss it?" Bree thrust a hand into her hair and tried to tuck it behind her ear. "You mean, you're not going to come up with an offer she can't refuse?"

"Very funny. You want to do comedy or talk about what to do when we reach *Signora* Massini's house?"

She sighed, put her hand to her temple and rubbed it. The long flight, the longer day, had left her with a headache.

"Talk," she said wearily. "What else do you know about the *signora?*"

Gianni shook his head. "Not much. Just what I've told you."

"So, the reason Tommy and Karen didn't name her as their baby's guardian was that Tommy didn't like her?"

"That, and the fact that Lucia is an American citizen. They'd have wanted her raised in her own country."

"Well, I can't see how the *signora* could disagree with that."

Gianni looked at Bree. "In a logical world, she wouldn't. Unfortunately, it isn't a logical world."

"It would be, if you ran it."

"What's that supposed to mean?"

"Oh, you know. Everything would be done just so. A schedule for this, another for that."

"There's nothing wrong with order."

"There's nothing wrong with spontaneity."

"Is that why you can't hold down a job?"

"Is that why you want to run my life?"

They looked at each other. Then Gianni laughed. "Oil and water," he said. "You and me. I don't know what

Karen and Tomasso were thinking when they chose us as guardians.'' He stepped on the gas and shot past another vehicle. ''I think our best approach to Grandma is going to be a cautious one. Let her set the pace until we know what's in her head.''

''Won't she come right out and tell us?''

''This is Sicily, Briana. Old customs still prevail.''

If *The Godfather* theme floated through her head one more time, Bree figured she was going to owe royalties to the guy who'd written it.

''Are we back to little old ladies in black?''

''We're back to facts. Fact one, Tommy didn't like her. That's saying a lot. He was the kind of guy who loved everybody. Fact two. Tommy's attorney has already given us fair warning.''

''Which you only just decided to share with me.''

''Fact three,'' Gianni said, ignoring the taunt, ''it'll be best if you follow my lead.''

''Fact four,'' she replied, glaring at him as she tucked back a strand of hair, ''have you forgotten our agreement? We make decisions together.''

''Damn it, woman, must we fight every step? I'm only suggesting we stick to the old adage. When in Rome...''

''You mean, when in Sicily, men are men and women are good for only one thing.''

He wanted to tell her she was good for lots of things. She was smart, she had a glib tongue—he was even starting to enjoy their arguments—but that, definitely, she had a special talent for that one thing...

But he wasn't stupid.

''Look,'' he said patiently, ''there are things we can say to soften her up. For instance, we can tell her we'll bring Lucia to Sicily for summer visits.''

That sounded reasonable. ''Fine.''

"We'll assure the *signora* that Lucia will learn her native language."

"Okay."

"And that you're going to learn it, too."

Bree looked at Gianni. "Gee," she said sweetly, "isn't this nice? You've already started following our new policy."

"My primary concern is that she might grab on to the fact that we're not married."

"Married?" She sat up straight and glared at him. "We're not even friends!"

"We were more than friends this morning."

It wasn't what he'd intended to say, but, damn it, did she have to keep putting her hands to her hair? Each time she did, her breasts lifted. Each time she moved in her seat, she came within an inch of brushing against his hand as he shifted. And what was that scent she was wearing? Jasmine? Tea Rose? Lily of the Valley?

"That," she said stiffly, "was an accident. I've forgotten all about it."

"The hell you have," he said gruffly.

"God, what an ego! I'm amazed there's room in this car for me."

The tires squealed as Gianni suddenly pulled to the side of the road and turned to her.

"You haven't forgotten this morning any more than I have," he said as he put the car in neutral and undid his seat belt.

Bree stared at him in alarm. "What do you think you're...? Gianni!" She slapped at his hands but he was quick. A second later, her belt was open and he was gathering her in his arms. "Damn it," she sputtered, "are you crazy? We don't have time—"

"We do," he said softly, his smile tilting. "We have all the time in the world for this."

And he kissed her.

It wasn't the way he'd kissed her before. If it had been, she knew she'd have fought, but this kiss was slow. Devastatingly slow. It was the way a man kisses a woman when he wants to seduce her. When he wants to excite her. When he wants her to know nothing is as important as this moment, this kiss.

Bree melted.

"Kiss me back," Gianni whispered against her mouth and she did, clasping his face, parting her lips, sucking on his tongue when he slid it between her teeth. He cupped her breast. His fingers brushed the nipple and she gasped, arched against him, felt the electricity streak from her breast to her belly to the place between her thighs that was already turning warm and wet. For him. Only for him.

She'd never felt this. Never wanted this. Never needed, needed, needed—

The headlights of an oncoming car caught them like a spotlight. Bree cried out and tore her mouth from Gianni's. He cupped her head, brought her face to the hollow of his throat but she pushed her hands against his chest and struggled until he let go of her.

"Briana," he said. "Briana…"

She shook her head. "Don't."

"Don't?" His voice roughened. He caught her by the shoulders, brought his face level with hers. "It's too late to play games, *cara*. I want you. You want me. We're adults. Why lie to ourselves and to each other?"

"Oh God," she whispered brokenly. "I don't know what's happening…"

"If it's any comfort," he said, with a harsh laugh, "neither do I." He pressed his lips to her temple. "I'm not going to apologize. I wanted to kiss you more than I've ever wanted anything in this world."

Bree reached out her hand as if to touch him, then pulled it back.

"We're complicating things," she whispered.

"Do you really think pretending we don't want to make love is going to uncomplicate them?"

"If—if we get involved, Gianni—if we do, what happens when we—when we end the relationship? We'll still have to deal with each other, because of Lucia."

He knew she was right. No matter what you said at the start of an affair, a man and a woman couldn't go from being lovers to being friends.

Yes. She was right. But what did that matter, when he wanted her so badly he ached? When he knew it was the same for her?

"Nobody can see the future, Bree."

"No. But we'd be fools not to try."

A muscle knotted in his jaw. He thought about taking her in his arms, kissing her until she stopped thinking. Putting his mouth on her breasts, sucking the nipples until she cried out with pleasure. Slipping his hand between her thighs, under her panties, stroking her until she came apart in his arms, until she begged him to unzip his trousers, lift her into his lap so she could lower herself on him, impale herself on him, take him deep, deep, deep...

Damn it, he was driving himself crazy!

Gianni sat back, fastened his seat belt and put the Ferrari in gear.

"Buckle up," he said sharply.

She did. He checked for traffic, pulled onto the road and wished to hell he could grab Tomasso by the collar and shake him.

Hey, paisano, he'd say, *look what you've done! There was, leading a perfectly normal life and then...*

And then?

Then, he'd met Briana. And she'd turned his world upside down.

CHAPTER SEVEN

THEY MISSED the turn-off twice before they doubled back and found it.

It wasn't a road at all but an old cart track that wound up the side of the mountain. In minutes, they were deep within an overgrown forest, tree branches whipping past only inches away.

Gianni put up the convertible top.

"Lovely road," Bree said lightly.

"Just great," he said through his teeth. He cursed at a particularly deep rut, shifted gears and slowed the car's speed until they were almost crawling.

"Maybe we ended up taking the wrong turn-off after all," Bree said, clutching the dashboard for leverage.

"The only other one we found was a dead end, remember? Besides, there's no going back. There's nowhere to turn around."

"Why would anybody want to live on a road like this?"

"To keep visitors out."

"How nice. Thank you for that encouraging thought, *Signore* Firelli."

Gianni flashed her a smile. "My pleasure, Miss O'Connell."

Bree grabbed for the door handle as the car lurched over another series of bumps.

"Seriously, if this road, or whatever you want to call it, is a measure of *Signora* Massini's hospitality, it's just one more reason to dislike her."

"Let's try to reserve judgment, okay?"

"That doesn't sound very lawyerly to me."

"Just goes to prove you don't know much about lawyers."

"One of my brothers is a lawyer. He never reserves judgment. Cullen always knows what's right and wrong." Bree looked at Gianni. "Sound familiar?" she said with saccharine charm.

"This is a different situation," Gianni said. He didn't really believe it, but he figured it wouldn't hurt to start with an open mind. "Maybe Tomasso's attorney got the wrong vibes. Maybe Tomasso had some personal thing that made him dislike the old lady. Maybe—"

"Maybe that's the house."

Gianni stuck his head out the window to get a better view. "Oh, damn," he said softly.

Damn, indeed. The house, outlined against the rapidly lightening sky, was still a distance away but even from here, Bree could see that it was enormous.

"You said it wouldn't be a castle."

"And I was wrong. It looks like something relocated from Transylvania."

"Want to change your upbeat take on what kind of friendly reception is waiting for us?"

Bree's tone was casual but Gianni wasn't buying it. He reached for her hand and enfolded it in his.

"Scared?" he said softly.

"No." She hesitated. "Terrified."

"Don't be." He brought her hand to his lips. "The law is on our side, remember?"

"Do you expect anybody who lives in a place like this to worry about the law?"

Gianni grinned. "*Signora* Massini is hardly the bride of Dracula."

"Maybe not, but if I see bats flying around the front door, I'm going to scream."

"*Cara.* The *signora* is only human."

"Right. But it's—it's like a one-two punch, you know? Meeting her. And meeting Lucia." Bree turned to him. "I think that's what really has me worried. Meeting our— our— What do you call a child when you're her guardian?"

"You call her a tremendous responsibility. And, to be honest, I'm as wary of what comes next as you are."

"I can't imagine you afraid of anything."

"Not of the *signora.* No matter what trouble she gives us, assuming she gives us any, we can handle her. But the baby… That's another story. What I told you before is true. I don't know a thing about children."

"We'll be okay as long as we don't let her figure that out."

"Tomasso's grandmother?"

"The baby." Bree smiled. "Cassie—my brother Keir's wife—Cassie said that was the way she got through giving their baby the first bath. She said she was terrified, but everything was okay because the baby didn't know it."

"Sounds like good advice for dealing with Lucia as well as the *signora.*"

"You're pretty smart when you want to be, Firelli."

"Mark this day down," Gianni said solemnly. "Briana O'Connell gives Gianni Firelli a compliment."

"Just don't let it go to your head."

"It won't." He sighed, let go of her hand and shifted gears as they emerged from the trees into the clearing. "That might be the last compliment you ever give me, *cara,* considering that I don't have a clue as to what we're walking into."

"Why does that sound so ominous?" Bree said, trying for a light touch and failing miserably.

He pulled the car over. "By now, Tomasso's grandmother has had time to think things over."

"Is that good or bad?"

Gianni shrugged. "Damned if I know. I suppose she could welcome us warmly. It's a long shot, but it's possible."

"So is snow in August."

"If she does, we'll stay for a few hours, get some sleep, give her a chance to say her goodbyes to the baby and then head for the airport."

"And if she's not glad to see us? What do we do then?"

He gave a long sigh. "I'm not sure. Postponing the inevitable might be a mistake."

"Meaning, we should take Lucia and leave right away."

"Yes—assuming that's a viable possibility."

"Why wouldn't it be? The will—"

"We don't want to make it look as if we're kidnapping the baby."

"We wouldn't be. The will—"

"We're in Sicily, not the United States. I told you, the customs—"

"Are different," Bree said impatiently. "I heard you. Still, the law is the law."

"Amazing," Gianni said wryly. "Here I am, a realist, trying to make you, an idealist, understand that there are times the law isn't all that matters."

"Is that what you think I am? An idealist?"

"I think you're a dreamer, *cara*." He lifted her hand to his mouth. "That you've spent your life searching for something you still haven't found." His eyes met hers. "Am I right?"

Bree stared at him. What were they talking about? Not Tomasso's grandmother. Not the baby. Then, what? Was Gianni thinking about what had happened a little while ago? Had she given it all away then? Did he know that nothing in her life had prepared her for what he made her feel when she was in his arms? That each time she looked at him, she wanted—she wanted—

Light poured into the car, blinding them. Bree screamed; Gianni said something quick and harsh in Italian and flung his door open. There were sounds of scuffling.

The light went out.

When her eyes finally adjusted to the greyness of the emerging dawn light, Bree saw Gianni struggling with a monster at least ten feet tall. She sprang from the car, grabbed a rock and raised it as high as she could.

"Stop it," she yelled, and swung with all her might. The monster staggered and dropped at her feet.

Bree hardly glanced at him. Instead she threw herself into Gianni's arms.

"Gianni? Gianni, are you all right?"

"I'm fine."

"Let me see." She ran her fingers over his face, checking for cuts. "I was so scared! I thought you—I thought it—"

Gianni caught her hands and pressed a quick kiss to them.

"I'm fine, *cara*." He knelt down beside the man, picked up the flashlight he'd dropped and switched it on. "Let's see if we can say the same for our friend."

"He was trying to hurt you."

"No," Gianni said gently, "he was talking to me."

"But—but I saw his hands and arms going in all directions."

"There's an old joke among my people," Gianni said dryly. "Tie up our hands and we'd be tongue-tied." He turned his attention to the huddled form on the ground. *"Siete tutto il di destra?"*

Bree stared at the monster, who no longer appeared to be ten feet tall. Nowhere even close to that. The reality of what had happened, what she'd done, hit home. "Oh God," she said shakily. "Is he—did I—?"

The man on the ground groaned and felt his head.

"*Signore?*"

Gianni nodded. "*Si. Chi sono voi?*"

"*Sono il maggiordomo di Signora Massini.*" He groaned again and touched his fingers to his head. "*Che cosa è accaduto? Che cosa lo ha colpito?*"

This time, it was Gianni who groaned.

"What did he say? Who is he?"

He ignored her and rattled off what she knew were more questions. The fallen monster answered. Gianni nodded. Then he looked at Bree.

"Take his other arm. Help me get him to his feet."

Bree squatted beside the man and put a hand under his elbow. "*Grazie,*" he said in a shaky voice. No, she thought, worrying her lip with her teeth as they stood him erect. Not ten feet. Not eight. Five, maybe. Only maybe.

"Do you speak English?" Gianni said.

"*Si, signore. Uno piccolo.* A little."

"I'm going to put you in my car and drive you to the house. All right?"

"Yes. *Grazie.* Thank you." The man put his hand to his head again. "What hit me?"

Bree opened her mouth. Gianni shook his head as he carefully handed him into the car.

"I'm not sure. A tree branch, perhaps. This area, where the road comes out of the woods... It needs attention."

"*Si.* I will speak with the gardener."

"You do that," Gianni said, and shut the door.

"Gianni? What's going on?"

Gianni sighed. He looked up to the pale cream of the morning sky and thought about how simple and predictable his life had been until yesterday.

"They saw our headlights from the house. When the lights stopped moving, the *signora* decided either we'd broken down or we were the press, trying to sneak in."

"The press? But why would the press—"

"I don't know. I suppose the accident made the local papers. The *signora* is something of an important figure, or so it would seem."

"So—so who's this man?"

Gianni's mouth thinned. "He's the butler."

"The—"

"The butler. You bashed the butler in the head."

Bree slapped her hand against her heart. "Ohmygod!"

"Indeed," Gianni said dryly.

"But I thought—I thought he was trying to—to hurt you…"

Her eyes were enormous, her hair was wild and she was trembling. Gianni felt his throat constrict. He wanted to tell Briana something but he wasn't sure what it was. Instead he whispered her name and pulled her into his arms.

"Thank you," he said gruffly.

"For what?" She gave a shaky laugh. "I thought I was taking out the Frankenstein monster. Instead I creamed the *signora's* butler. That's a heck of a way to start our visit, don't you think?"

"Well, it was impressive." He smiled, then pressed a kiss in her hair and held her at arm's length. "She'll never know."

"You think?"

"I know," he said firmly. "A tree branch. That's what did it."

Bree sighed. "Okay."

"You swing a mean rock, *cara.*"

She grinned. "I grew up with three brothers. We played baseball a lot."

He smiled back and brushed her hair from her eyes. "Baseball, huh?"

"Sure. Keir taught me."

"Did he teach you to take on monsters, too?"

"Cullen taught me that," she said, laughing softly.

"What about driving shift cars? Any of your brothers give you those lessons?"

"Of course," she said primly. "Sean."

"Remind me to thank them when I meet them."

"Will you?" Bree said, her smile tilting. "Meet my brothers, I mean?"

Of course he would. Years of dealing with each other stretched ahead of them. In all that time, they'd be bound to step into each other's lives.

But that wasn't what she was thinking. Neither was he. She was thinking of the feeling growing between them, one that seemed to have a power all its own.

A muscle knotted in Gianni's cheek. "Of course," he said softly. "I'll have to tell them how brave their sister is."

"And stupid. I can't believe I attacked the butler."

"For what it's worth, I attacked him, too."

"You didn't conk him in the head."

Gianni laughed. "No. I didn't." He tilted Bree's chin up. "You were brave, *cara*. Now, I'm going to ask you to be brave again."

"How?"

"By meeting Tomasso's grandmother alone."

Bree blinked. "What?"

"The Ferrari won't hold all of us, and I'm not about to let you walk all the distance through this meadow alone."

"Don't be silly. What could possibly hurt me?"

"Wild boars," he said, with no smile at all. "Wild dogs. You can find both in these mountains. You'll drive, Briana. I'll walk."

"But—but—"

"Just don't get into conversation with the *signora* until I get there. I'll only be a few minutes behind you." Gianni's hands slipped to her shoulders. "Stick to the basics. Introduce yourself. Tell her you're pleased to meet her. Tell her I'll be right along.''

"Tell her I beaned the butler and oh, by the way, I've come to take her great-grandchild.''

"A tree branch beaned the butler," he said evenly. "And you've come to do the bidding of the last will and testament of our friends. But there'll be no need to tell her that. All you have to do is be polite and mark time until I arrive.''

"You mean, you want me to do the old Sicilian female thing. Listen, nod my head and smile.''

"You couldn't do the old Sicilian female thing, such as it is, if your life depended on it.''

Bree sighed. "I know. I just don't…'' She cast a glance over her shoulder. The huge grey stone house, looming cold and desolate on a hill, was fully visible now. "Ugh. I can see why Tomasso didn't want his baby raised here.''

"And we've yet to meet the *signora*,'' Gianni said grimly.

"You said it wouldn't be a castle, and it isn't.'' She gave a nervous laugh. "Did I say I was worried about bats? Vampires might be the real bet.''

Gianni cupped her face, bent to her and brushed his mouth lightly over hers.

"Get going,'' he whispered. "Just remember, if things get tough, all you have to do is get the lady into the noonday sun and we'll be fine.''

Bree smiled, as he'd hoped she would.

"See you in five, Firelli,'' she said airily.

Then she got into the Ferrari, ground the gears hard enough to turn Gianni's face white, patted the arm of the man seated beside her and drove off, while Gianni trudged after the car.

It didn't pay to listen to the sounds the clutch made.

It didn't pay to wonder what *Signora* Massini would think when she saw her wounded butler. He was pretty sure she

wouldn't buy the tree branch story, but would she figure ou
that Bree had tried to brain the man?

A smile curved his mouth.

His Briana was quite a woman. Strong. Resilient. And, a
the same time, soft. Sweet. Vulnerable. Yes, indeed, his Bri
ana…

Gianni blinked.

His Briana? What kind of thinking was that? He like
her. Liked her a lot, which was saying quite a bit when yo
considered he'd thought her the curse of all womanhoo
only a day ago, but she wasn't his. There wasn't a woma
on the planet he'd ever thought of as "his" and ther
wouldn't be, not for years and years and years.

This was sex. Okay. Sex and like. Liking. Whatever i
hell the word was, Gianni thought irritably as he plodde
toward the house. He could want Bree and like her at th
same time, couldn't he? So what if what he felt for her wa
different?

Not that he'd ever gone to bed with a woman he didn'
like. The truth was, he had to like a woman before h
wanted her. Well, no. Bree was the exception to that. Wha
he'd felt for her initially hadn't been anything positive…

But he'd wanted her anyway.

"Hell," Gianni muttered.

Okay. It was time to take a step back. Return, as it were
to logic. Get the baby. Go home to the States. Get Brian
and the child settled in next door, hire a nanny, organiz
things so they ran smoothly and then slip back into his ow
life…

"…wouldn't feel the way he did! You are an impossi
ble—"

The breeze swept the rest of the words away, but it didn'
matter. Gianni knew the voice was Bree's.

He stopped in his tracks.

"No," he said under his breath, "please, no."

The house was only a few yards away. He winced at the sight of the Ferrari parked, more or less, with its front tires drunkenly perched on the base of a set of wide flagstone steps.

The butler, poor man, was nowhere in sight.

Two women held center stage. One was a tall, imposing figure leaning on a silver cane.

The other was Briana. And from the way she was gesturing as her hair swirled around her face, he knew damned well she'd forgotten everything he'd told her.

CHAPTER EIGHT

GIANNI TOOK a deep breath, forced a smile to his lips and bounded up the steps.

"Briana," he said cheerfully. "You made excellent time." She swung around and glared at him. He returned a warning look, then smiled again as he extended his hand to the *signora,* who pointedly ignored it. "*Signora* Massini. *Buon giorno. Com'è sta? Mi dispiace sono in ritardo, mai—*"

"What are you telling her?" Bree demanded.

It wasn't easy, but Gianni kept his smile. "Calm down," he said through his teeth.

"I asked you a question. What did you just say?"

Gianni flashed another smile at the stiff-faced *signora.* "*Signora. Uno momento, per favore.*" His smile vanished as he grabbed Bree's wrist and pulled her aside. "I said hello, for God's sake. Hello, how are you, I'm sorry I'm late."

"You're sorry *we're* late," Bree snapped, "or has that 'we make decisions together' thing already gone by the wayside?"

"Bree. Take it easy. I don't know what's happening here, but—"

"What is happening," the *signora* said, her voice icy enough to put a layer of frost on the rapidly lightening day, "is that your companion chooses not to understand what she's been told."

"You mean, you speak English?" Bree said hotly. She

swung toward Gianni. "She pretended she couldn't. Only one sentence. That's all she kept repeating. 'You are not welcome here.' That was what she said, over and over and—"

"It was all it is necessary to say. Unfortunately your companion refuses to believe it."

Gianni could feel his smile slipping. He hadn't expected a warm welcome but he certainly hadn't anticipated being turned away at the door. And then there was the intonation Tomasso's grandmother had twice put on the word "companion..."

"We've come a long way, *signora*. Surely this isn't an example of Sicilian hospitality."

"I am not Sicilian, *Signore* Firelli, as you can surely discern from my speech. I am Roman, brought to this godforsaken island by my late husband."

"Not Sicilian," Bree snorted. "She's lived here for, what, a hundred years?"

"Bree," Gianni said tightly, "let me handle this."

"I am sorry you've made a long trip for nothing, *signore*."

"Does she call coming for Karen's and Tommy's baby 'nothing?'"

"Bree, damn it, will you keep quiet?"

"If you choose not to teach this girl her place, I shall."

That did it. Gianni gave up the smile and any attempt at cordiality. "This is Briana O'Connell. She was Karen's closest friend and, as you well know, she is now Lucia's guardian."

"She has been given that title, yes. As have you."

"Right. And unless you want to face us in court, I suggest you step aside and let us in."

The *signora* smiled. "An empty threat, *signore*. This is Sicily. Things move slowly here." She took a step back.

"If we ever do meet in court, it won't be for years and years. Now you will excuse me. I have things to do."

"Tomasso's attorney has friends in high places," Gianni said. It wasn't really a lie. Every lawyer had, or thought he had, friends in high places, but this woman didn't have to know that. "And I have contacts, too. Contacts in the press." That, at least, was true. He was a Federal prosecutor. He'd handled cases that dripped with notoriety. He'd never given so much as a nod to any of the dozens of reporters who'd begged for exclusives but if he had to, he would now. "I wonder what those who live on what you refer to as this godforsaken island would say about a wealthy woman who believes she's above the law."

"Oh, she's wealthy, all right," Bree said. "Look at this house. This—this Frankenstein's castle where she thinks she has a chance in hell of raising our baby—"

Our baby. The words made Gianni's heart stop. He looked at the fire in Bree's eyes, grasped her hand and wound his fingers through hers.

"Your choice, *signora*. We do this the easy way—or we do it in public."

There was a beat of silence. Then the *signora* rapped her cane sharply on the fieldstone. The butler Bree had slugged appeared behind her. He looked fine, Gianni saw with relief, if you didn't pay attention to the lump on his head.

"Bartolemo. Get their luggage. Put it in the blue bedroom."

"Thank you," Gianni said politely.

"For what?" The *signora's* smile was sly. "For agreeing to speak with you?" She paused. "Or for putting you in one bedroom? Your lack of morality is not my affair, *Signore* Firelli, not unless it impacts my great-granddaughter. I promise you, I will not let that happen."

And that, Gianni thought as they followed her into the

cavernous foyer, that was the situation they faced, neatly packaged in the proverbial nutshell.

THE BLUE ROOM was enormous, with furniture to suit. The ceiling was at least twelve feet high and decorated with cherubs and harps. Silk draperies hung against the windows and enclosed the four-poster bed. It was a room filled with what were surely priceless antiques and centuries of history.

Bree hated it on sight.

"It's got all the vitality of a corpse," she said, as soon as Bartolemo bowed himself into the hall and shut the door. "This whole house is like a graveyard."

"I'd say it was more like a museum," Gianni said, yanking off his jacket and tossing it on a chair, "but I won't argue with your definition."

"And that woman. Who does she think she is?"

Gianni, who'd taken in stories about what peasants could expect from Italian aristocracy with his mother's milk, laughed.

"She knows who she is, *cara. Signora* Emma Olivia Gracia Massini."

"You know what I mean."

"I know exactly what you mean," he said, flinging his necktie after the jacket. "Trouble is, she's probably right. She's a powerful woman."

Bree looked at him. "Are you telling me she can win? That she can keep the baby, despite the terms of the will?"

"She can delay things interminably, if she chooses."

"But you faced her down. You got us through the door."

Gianni sat down on the bed. The endless hours, the upheaval in his life, were suddenly catching up with him.

"I threatened her with publicity. It's the last thing members of *la famiglia* want."

Bree's eyes widened. "*Signora* Massini is—"

"Her husband was. I knew I'd heard the name before,

but when I saw this house, when she said her husband had brought her here from Rome…'' He plumped the pillows behind him, yawned and sat back. ''Publicity's our ace in the hole, *cara*.''

''I thought the law was our ace in the hole.''

''Yes, but she's right about how long it would take for this to wind through the courts.''

''What about all those contacts Tommy's attorney has?''

Gianni sighed. ''Who knows? At this point, I'm only sure of two things. The *signora* wants to avoid publicity—and she doesn't want her great-granddaughter raised by a pair of immoral Americans.''

He could almost see Briana bristle. ''Speak for yourself, Firelli. I am not immoral.''

''You're not married.''

''Neither are you.''

''We're going to be Lucia's guardians but we're male and female.''

''A brilliant observation.''

''And we're not married to each other.'' Gianni's eyes met hers; a slow, sexy smile tilted across his mouth. ''Who knows where that might lead?''

Bree felt her cheeks heat but she kept her gaze steady on his. ''It won't lead us anywhere. Not again. I told you, things are complicated enough without—''

''I know. I agree. I'll find a solution, but first I need some sleep.''

She seemed to notice the one enormous bed for the very first time. ''Why did she put us in here?'' she said crossly. ''When she said the blue suite, I thought it meant we'd have two bedrooms.''

''It's her way of telling us she knows we're lovers.''

''But we're not.''

''What a short memory you have, *cara*.''

Bree slapped her hands on her hips. ''We are not lovers,''

she said firmly. "I'm going to go downstairs, find the *signora* and tell her—"

"We'll tell her something, but not now." Gianni yawned. "We have to get some sleep or the *signora* will dance rings around us."

He was right. Bree could feel exhaustion seeping through her bones. "All right. I'll take a nap in that chair."

"Don't be ridiculous." He patted the bed. "Lie down here."

"In the same bed as you?" She folded her arms. "No way."

"The bed is the size of a football field. You take one side. I'll take the other. You won't even know we're sharing it."

"No."

"Oh, for God's sake!" He was off the bed and beside her before she could react. She squealed as he lifted her in his arms, carried her to the bed and dumped her on it. "Close your eyes," he said sternly. "Go to sleep." He grabbed her when she tried to get up. "You're staying put, O'Connell."

"I'm not the least bit tired."

"You're out on your feet." Gianni stretched out beside her. "Close your eyes. Go to sleep. I don't want you going near the *signora* again without me."

"I don't take orders from you. How come you keep forgetting that?"

"I'm Sicilian. I know the customs here."

"I'm an intelligent woman. I can figure them out."

"Oh, yeah," he said sarcastically, "I could tell that after watching how well you handled *la signora*."

Bree glared at the ceiling. "She's an awful person."

"She's the person we have to deal with."

"I want to see the baby."

"Me, too." Well, that was a lie. Why would he want to

see the baby when he was terrified of even touching it? Something so small. So fragile. So dependent. So determined to change his life for years and years to come. "But we need some sleep first."

"I want to see her now."

Bree started to move. Gianni turned on his side, wrapped an arm around her waist and pulled her back against him.

"Get over here."

"Let go!"

"Damn it, do not fight me on this!"

"You said you'd take one side of the bed and I'd take the other. You said—"

"Shut up, *cara*."

"I am not tired!"

"Yeah, well, I am."

There was a brief silence. "My clothes will get wrinkled."

Tired as he was, he almost laughed. "The last resort of a desperate woman," he said. "Put your head on the pillow. Go to sleep."

"You can force me to lie here, but you can't force me to sleep."

"No," he said wearily, "I can't. Just keep this in mind. I'm a light sleeper. You try to get away, I'll know it."

"Bastard," she huffed.

Gianni, the light sleeper, answered with a snore.

Bree lay stiff under the weight of his encircling arm. They were tucked against each other like a pair of spoons.

She ground her teeth together.

All those promises about decisions and the minute they were confronted by the *signora,* they flew out the window.

He was right when he'd said he liked taking care of women. And she was almost ready to admit—never to him, of course—that she could see why women liked having him take care of them. Being in his arms, his body hard and warm against hers, his breath soft in her hair, she couldn't think of a place she'd rather be.

Still, she wouldn't sleep. Never. Not like this. Not like...

Bree's lashes brushed her cheeks. Seconds later, safe in Gianni's embrace, she was asleep.

LONG SHADOWS slanted across the bed.

Gianni opened his eyes. Late afternoon? Had he really slept that long? He yawned, stretched...and felt the warmth of a woman's body pressed tightly against his.

Bree.

She was sound asleep but sometime during their nap, she'd turned toward him. Now she lay in his arms, her head nestled against his shoulder, one hand on his chest, one leg flung across his. She'd wrapped herself around him despite all those protests about sharing the bed.

She felt soft, smelled sweet, looked young and trusting and more beautiful than any woman he'd ever known.

Gianni felt his heart turn over.

Gently he shifted his weight until she lay even closer in his arms. She sighed, and the whisper was like a caress against his throat.

She was more than beautiful.

He smiled. He knew she wouldn't think so. Her hair was what women called a mess. He thought sleep-tousled curls were sexy. There was a dark smudge of mascara below one eye and her lipstick, pale to begin with, had completely worn off.

Gianni's arms tightened around her.

She was a tough woman, his Briana. At least, that was what she wanted the world to think. He knew differently. She had a softness, a delicacy that left her vulnerable. She needed someone to protect her. To keep the world at bay. To hold her and comfort her.

She needed—she needed...

"Mmm."

Bree's eyelids fluttered. She sighed again, stretched against him as delicately as a cat. Her body curved against his, her breasts warm against his chest, her hips arching into him.

She was going to be upset when she came fully awake and realized she was lying in his arms, that they were sharing the same space, that her mouth was close enough for him to kiss.

Her eyes opened. Confusion clouded the deep blue irises. "Gianni?" she murmured, and he did what any man would do in that situation.

He kissed her.

She stiffened. She was going to push him away and, damn it, she had every right. He'd promised not to touch her, agreed that this—this attraction, whatever you wanted to call it, could only complicate a situation that was already impossible.

But then she made a little humming sound, curled her arms around his neck and her mouth, her sweet-as-honey mouth, opened to his.

Gianni groaned and deepened the kiss.

Her body arched against his. Her hand cupped his jaw.

"Briana," he whispered, and kissed her throat.

"Yes," she said, "yes. Oh, yes."

He rolled her onto her back, kissed her throat again. Her blouse was in the way; he tried to undo the top button but his hands were shaking and finally he growled with frustration, grasped the silk lapels and tore it open.

She wore a white cotton bra. He'd been with women who bought their lingerie with sex on their minds. This was the least erotic thing he'd ever seen, yet it turned his already-hard erection to steel. The swell of her breasts above the bra was a line so delicately feminine he felt his throat constrict.

He bent his head, kissed that curve, kissed one breast, then the other. Bree sobbed his name, buried her hands in his hair and brought his mouth to hers.

He lingered over the kiss.

Alone in the universe, there was time to do what he had not done yesterday morning.

Time to savor the sweetness of her mouth.

The silk of her skin.

The taste of her nipples on his tongue.

When she whispered his name, there was time to let the music of it echo inside him.

And when she touched him, God, when she touched him, moving her hands over his face, his shoulders; slipping them under his shirt so he felt their heat against his bare skin...

Gianni gritted his teeth.

He wanted this to last forever.

"Slowly," he said, when her hand dropped lower. "Slowly," he groaned when she cupped his erection and sent him too close to the edge. It killed him to clasp her hand and lift it from him but he did it, brought it to his mouth, sucked her fingers, pressed an open-mouthed kiss to the center of her palm even though he longed to tear off the rest of her clothes.

He wouldn't.

It had all gone too quickly that first time. This time would be slow. It would be for her.

It would be because he had never wanted a woman as he wanted Briana.

He bent to her, kissed her mouth, her throat, put his lips to her breast and nipped the beaded flesh outlined beneath the soft white cotton. She moaned and he kissed her again so that her sweet, hot little cries became part of him. He sat her up, undid the clasp of her bra. She caught it as it fell away from her and he shook his head, caught her wrists, bared her breasts to his eyes.

Ah, dear God, her breasts. Her beautiful, beautiful breasts. They were small, high, the color of cream, the crests budded flowers of deepest rose. He cupped them, kissed them, swept his thumbs across the tips.

Her eyes darkened.

"Do you like the feel of my hands on you?" he said. "Tell me. Tell me what you like."

"That," she said as he ran his fingers over her nipples again. "Oh, that. That…"

He sucked one nipple into his mouth and then the other, and she cried out in passion. Gianni licked her, teased her with his tongue. Then he brought his lips to hers and kissed her while he caressed her.

When she was sobbing in his arms, he lay her back against the pillows.

"Briana," he whispered, "Briana…"

There was more to say, but he didn't have the words. Controlling himself took all his strength.

"Touch me," she whispered, and he came close to forgetting all his good intentions.

He pushed up her skirt, slipped his hand between her thighs. Her panties were already wet; he bit back a groan as he fought the desire to unzip his trousers and bury himself deep inside her.

This was for her. All for her.

He pulled her panties down and watched her face as he stroked her. Her eyes blurred but they stayed on his.

"Gianni," she sobbed. "Gianni…"

Gently he parted the delicate female flesh. Sought the bud within. Found it, caressed it and with a soft cry, she came apart in his arms. He drew her tightly against him, running his hand down her back, stroking her face, dropping soft kisses on her hair, rocking her against him until she stopped trembling and her breathing steadied.

Then he cupped her face and lifted it to him.

Her skin was flushed, her lips parted. She looked like a woman who had been well-loved and his heart flooded with some new, unknown emotion.

"Are you all right, *cara?*" he whispered.

She nodded and slicked the tip of her tongue across her bottom lip. "I'm sorry," she whispered. "Gianni, I'm so—"

He stopped her words with a kiss.

"It's what I wanted," he said softly. "I wanted to see you come for me."

"But—but what about you? That wasn't—it couldn't have been enough."

He shook his head and silenced her with another kiss.

"It was everything," he said gruffly.

The damnedest thing was, it was true. His heart still pounded, his body still ached with need, but nothing he'd ever done with a woman before this had ever left him with such a profound feeling of completion.

She smiled and burrowed closer.

Seconds later, he felt her relax. Her breathing slowed. She was asleep.

Her head was on his shoulder. He could feel the muscle starting to complain but an aching muscle was a small price to pay for what had just happened.

For what was happening, though he'd be damned if he knew what it was.

Bree murmured something. It sounded like his name. Gianni hoped it was.

He drew her even closer.

Lying here was a mistake. It was time to get up, take a shower, find the kitchen in this drafty old pile of stone and get a cup of coffee. *Espresso,* the more super-charged the better. He had to think about what to do next, how to get the baby away from the *signora* without ending up mired in legal quicksand.

Back home, stuff like this could drag on forever. From what he knew of the law here, forever might be just the beginning.

He'd only delayed things by threatening publicity. The *signora,* he was sure, would figure a way around that soon enough.

Her threat about morality was the problem.

Unless things had changed in these little hill towns, the idea that a baby of Sicilian descent was going to be raised by a man and women who weren't married would be anathema.

If she played it right, the *signora* could come out of this a local saint, intent on maintaining the moral code.

Gianni sighed.

Nothing was clear yet. He was still too wiped out to think straight.

Gently, he kissed Bree's mouth. Then he drifted off to sleep.

WHAT WOKE HIM this time wasn't the softness of Bree in his arms.

It was a blast of light.

He opened his eyes, cursed softly and screwed them shut again.

"Hey," he said, struggling up against the pillows, "turn that thing off."

"Get up, Firelli."

Cautiously he opened his eyes again. Briana was standing at the foot of the bed. She'd showered—her hair was damp and curling on her shoulders—and changed her clothes.

She'd changed her mood, too, judging by her unsmiling face.

He swung his legs to the floor and ran his hands through his hair. "What's the matter?"

"Oh, nothing. Nothing except the fact that we've wasted the entire day, thanks to you."

"Bree. Wait a minute…"

"And we've done exactly what that old witch wanted us to do, also thanks to you."

Gianni's head came up. "Huh?"

"She put us in this room to drive home a point. You said so yourself."

Had he said that? His head was fuzzy. When was the last time they'd eaten? Better still, when was the last time he'd had a jolt of caffeine? Damned if he didn't need one now to clear his brain.

"Cara," he said carefully, "I'm not following you. What point?"

"That we're—we're lovers."

Color rose in her face. Seeing it made him shake his head.

"We *are* lovers. Besides, what does that have to do with anything?"

"We are not lovers. We're—we're two people who took a complicated situation and made it worse after we agreed we wouldn't."

"Briana." He got to his feet and walked toward her. "Listen to me. Just because we made love—"

"I don't want to talk about this now. I want to see Lucia."

"And we will. But your attitude—"

"I don't have an attitude, Firelli."

And pigs could fly. "Bree," he said, striving to stay calm, *"cara…"*

"Will you stop calling me that?" she said, slapping his hands away as he reached for her. "Just get yourself ready so we can go find the *signora.*"

Gianni's eyes narrowed. "I don't know what's going on in your head, Briana, but I don't like it."

"That really breaks my heart."

"This discussion isn't over."

"I'll give you ten minutes. Then I'll go looking for the *signora* on my own."

"Do that," he said softly, "and I promise, you'll regret it."

Briana's chin lifted. "That's right. Go into macho mode. When in Sicily—"

"Watch what you say to me."

"Why? Will you beat me if I don't?"

A thin smile spread across his mouth. "I've got a much better way of bringing you to heel than that," he said, pulling her against him and crushing her mouth beneath his.

Bree wanted to sink into the kiss, wind her arms around his neck and lean into his warm, strong body.

Except, that would be playing right into his hands. It was what men like this expected of women. It was how they controlled them.

She slammed her hands on his arms, twisted her mouth away from his. "Stop it! Are you crazy? I just told you, that's over."

He looked into her eyes. "Is it?"

Gianni turned his back, strolled into the bathroom and shut the door. When she heard the shower come on, she sank back against the wall.

What had happened before wasn't only his fault. She had to admit that to herself, if not to him. But it wouldn't happen again.

Waking that second time, wrapped in Gianni's arms, remembering what she'd felt when he made love to her, the incandescent joy, the soaring wonder...

Terrifying. All of it.

That she, who knew better, would forget everything she knew about that kind of passion, was unbelievable. That she'd lose all sense of self was incredible. That she'd let a man gain such control over her was unbearable.

Her head drooped.

She had not signed on for any of this. Gianni was going to have to understand that. No way could they be Lucia's guardians until they sorted things out. They were not lovers. They would not be lovers. She would not let herself feel— let herself feel—

Someone knocked at the door.

Bree stood away from the wall, ran her fingers through her hair, touched her lips.

"Yes?"

A woman answered in what sounded like a babble of Sicilian. Bree only understood one word. *Bambino.*

It was enough.

She took a deep breath, opened the door and a woman in a white uniform handed her the tiny bundle that would forever change her life.

CHAPTER NINE

THE BABY was gorgeous.

She was also adorable, perfect, scrumptious and undoubtedly a genius, even at this tender age.

Bree, smitten by emotions new to her, could tell all that on sight.

By the time she'd followed the nurse down the stairs to a sitting room the size of a small theater, every fear she'd harbored about handling Lucia had been swept aside.

The baby lay in her arms as if she belonged there, gazed up at her face and instantly took control of Briana's heart.

The responsibility was still awesome, maybe even more so now that the moment of assuming it had actually arrived, but all her instincts told her she was more than capable of dealing with her new role.

As for the changes this would make in her life... They didn't matter. Whatever it took to raise this child, she would do. Gladly. Nothing she'd ever taken on had come close to seeming so right.

"We're going to get along just fine," she told the baby.

Lucia gurgled.

"I don't know a lot about babies but then, babies don't know a lot about grown-ups. We'll learn together."

Lucia regarded her solemnly, her chocolate-brown eyes wide and unblinking. Then she smiled and reached out a tiny hand to swat at Bree's chin.

Bree laughed, clasped the hand and gave a smacking kiss to each little finger.

"You're a sweetheart!" She looked at the nurse. "Lucia is—she is *mucho bella.*"

She'd probably gotten her languages confused but it didn't matter. The nurse, who'd been watching the proceedings with hawk-like intensity, visibly relaxed.

"Si, signorina. È un bambino meraviglioso."

"Gemma is right. Lucia is a wonderful child."

Bree swung around. *Signora* Massini stood in the doorway, unsmiling, every hair in place, as formidable in appearance as she'd been that morning. She'd changed from her suit to a long black gown. Did the lady dress for dinner all the time, or was this another attempt at intimidation?

The answer came quickly enough. The *signora* did a slow visual appraisal, taking in Bree's damp, untamed curls, her linen trousers, T-shirt and sandals with a smile that could only be called condescending.

"It's in her genes. Some things apparently skip a generation, but good breeding will always win out."

To hell with you, Bree thought, and looked her straight in the eye.

"Yes. It does. After all, her mother and father were remarkable people."

The *signora's* mouth twisted. "My grandson was remarkable only in his selfish determination to live a life he preferred, and his wife was a nobody." The cane tapped lightly against the hardwood floor as she came toward Bree. "This child will not be like either of them."

"This child," Bree said coolly, "will be the person she chooses to be."

"An unfortunate American attitude."

"An exemplary *modern* attitude. And I suggest you keep your thoughts about Tommy and Karen to yourself, *Signora* Massini. I don't want to hear them."

"You won't have to, Miss O'Connell. You've had this time with Lucia before dinner and, if you wish, you may see her again before you leave in the morning.'' She smiled thinly. "I can keep my opinions to myself for that long."

The baby cooed happily. How was she to know the course of her life was being decided? Bree smiled down at the child, then brought her to her shoulder.

"We're not leaving without Lucia."

"And I am not giving her up."

"You don't have a choice. The will—"

"The will is a piece of paper. Attorneys are paid well to turn pieces of paper into confetti."

"They're paid even better to enforce the wishes of the people who wrote them."

Gianni smiled politely as he walked into the room. He'd lingered outside the door long enough to know that Bree was revving into full battle mode. That was the last thing he wanted.

The only way to win here was to outplay the *signora,* and a verbal battle wasn't going to do it.

"*Cara,*" he said, smiling at Bree. "Where did you go? I finished my shower and found our room empty."

Bree flushed. Was he crazy, talking so easily about their relationship?

"I wanted to see Lucia," she said stiffly.

"And here she is." Gianni looked at the baby. Big eyes, tiny nose, small mouth. That about exhausted all he knew of children this young. Bree was looking at him expectantly. Was he supposed to say something to this football-sized bundle? "Cute," he said gamely.

"She's adorable," Bree said, and gave the bundle the kind of smile she'd never yet given him.

"She is healthy," the *signora* said. "Her nurse takes excellent care of her."

Gianni held out his finger. The baby grabbed it, dragged it to her mouth and chomped down.

"She doesn't have any teeth!"

"She's too young to have teeth. See? She's smiling."
Briana smiled, too. "She likes you."

"At this age, a child has no likes or dislikes," *Signora*
Massini said coolly. "Not as we know them. Infants react
to stimuli. Heat, cold, hunger, whatever. Just now, Lucia
may have gas. To attribute complex emotions to babies is
ludicrous."

Bree stared at the woman. "Do you honestly believe
that?"

"It's scientific fact."

"No wonder Tommy didn't want you raising his child!"

"Briana," Gianni said quickly. "Why don't you let me
hold Lucia for a while?"

"With that sort of attitude," Bree said, ignoring him, "I
don't even know if we'll let Lucia visit you every summer."

"There will be no need for visits," the older woman
snapped. "Lucia will live here, with me."

Bree swung toward Gianni. "When are you going to tell
her she's out of line!"

"How about letting me hold the baby?" he said.

It wasn't what he'd intended to say and it sure as hell
wasn't what he wanted to do. The pale pink bundle scared
the bejeezus out of him. The kid was all big eyes and jerky
arm motion...and, oh man, was that a trickle of drool coming from one side of its mouth?

But he had to do something to keep Bree from going to
war. Bad enough she'd come down here alone, to face the
signora. Face her? Hell, she was baiting her and that was
the last thing that would be effective in dealing with a
woman who thought she owned the planet.

The only possible diversion was the baby.

"May I?" he said again, and held out his arms.

Bree looked at him warily. Didn't he look as if he knew
what he was doing? Gianni curved his lips in a smile.

"Hey, pussycat," he said.

That did it. Bree handed the kid over.

He took the transfer carefully, one hand on the baby's bottom, one curving around her back. She weighed more than he'd figured. More than a football, anyway.

"Support her head," Bree cautioned, and he nodded as if he'd known that all along while he adjusted his grip and cupped his hand over the baby's neck and the back of its head.

Not it. Her. This was a her.

A very small her.

She was also warm and sweet-smelling, though he couldn't quite place the scent.

"Baby powder," Bree said softly, and he realized he must have spoken aloud. "And you don't have to hold her like that."

"Like how?"

"Like she's made of glass. She won't break."

No? The kid looked as if she might, but people had been having and handling babies for thousands of years. Maybe they weren't as fragile as they seemed. Carefully he relaxed his grip and drew the bundle closer to his chest.

"Da," the baby said, and grinned.

"Look, she's smiling at you again."

"That is not a smile. It is gas."

Gas? Hell, no. The kid was definitely smiling.

"She has yet to smile at anyone. I assure you, what you see is not a smile."

Yes, indeed. It was a smile, no matter what the old witch said. Lucia was flashing him a wide, toothless grin.

"The child has never seen you before. Why would she smile?"

"Perhaps," he said pleasantly, "she recognizes the people who are going to raise her."

So much for not baiting the dragon but, hell, he wasn't going to let her get away with that. The baby was smiling, and if she'd never yet done such a thing before, one look at this house and this old woman and he understood the reason.

Signora Massini eyed him coldly. "This is a pointless argument. Give her back to her nurse, *Signore* Firelli. It is bedtime."

"Let me say goodnight," Bree said, and reached for the baby.

"Sure," he said softly, and put Lucia in her arms.

He watched as she bent her face to the child's. She was crooning something to her and the baby made a little gurgling sound of pleasure as she patted Bree's cheek.

Amazing.

They'd talked about this moment, about what it would be like when this baby, this bolt of lightning from out of a serene blue sky, finally came into their lives.

What did either of them know about babies? He'd expected to feel fear. Okay, terror the first time he held Lucia and he had. Briana had expressed the same doubts but watching her now, laughing as the baby tugged on her nose, he suddenly knew how right this was.

Karen and Tomasso had chosen well. Bree would make a wonderful guardian.

She'd make a wonderful mother.

He could almost see her holding another baby while a slightly older Lucia clung contentedly to his hand, except the new baby would have Bree's golden curls, her blue eyes...

Or they might be green, like his.

Gianni took a hurried step back.

"Briana," he said, "give the baby to her nurse."

"In a minute."

"Now."

She looked at him, her eyes narrowing in a way he knew was dangerous, and he forced a quick smile.

"We have important business to discuss with *Signora* Massini." He took a deep breath, told himself to slow down. "And, to tell the truth, I don't remember the last time we ate." He turned to the *signora* with a polite smile. "You are inviting us to dinner, aren't you?"

"Dinner tonight. Breakfast tomorrow." Tomasso's grandmother tapped her cane against the floor. "After that, *signore,* I am afraid we must part."

THE DINING ROOM made the sitting room seem cramped.

Twenty-four ladder-back chairs were lined up at a table that stretched through a room hung with tapestries. A fire blazed on a hearth Bree suspected might be big enough to hold her entire apartment. She'd thought the fire just another bit of pretension until they'd been seated and goose bumps rose on her arms.

It was summer outside. In here, it was winter.

Why not? she thought, desultorily shifting bits of cake from one part of her plate to another with her fork. This was another world, never mind another weather system.

The three of them were seated at one end of the table, the *signora* at the head, she and Gianni on either side. They'd eaten their meal in silence, all five courses, from tasteless consommé to tasteless dessert. No. Not true. Nobody had eaten. Instead they'd gone through the motions.

There'd been no conversation. She'd started to talk about the baby, and Gianni had tapped her foot with his. A while later, she'd opened her mouth again and before she'd gotten two words out, he'd tapped her foot again, harder this time, hard enough so she'd glared at him across the polished mahogany.

Now, her eyes flashed.

When I'm good and ready, his flashed back.

Oh, yes, they were handling this together, all right. She was furious at herself for deferring to Gianni but there was the one slim chance he was right, that he understood the medieval customs of this place and she didn't.

A silent maid tiptoed in and took away their dessert plates, then tiptoed back with a coffee service. The *signora* poured tiny cups of *espresso,* complete with tiny curls of lemon peel.

"Thank you," Bree said stiffly when the *signora* held out her coffee.

She took a sip. Thank God, this part of the meal was edible. And thank God the endless meal was coming to an end. If Gianni didn't say something soon—

"This is excellent *espresso,*" he said politely.

The *signora* inclined her head.

"And an excellent meal."

Another inclination of that elegant head.

"But it's time to discuss our situation."

The *signora* looked at him across her tiny cup. "We've already done that. I have no intention of accepting my grandson's will as legitimate."

"On what grounds will you contest it?"

She shrugged. "That is not my decision, it is my attorney's. There are several, ranging from the undue influence of Tomasso's wife—"

"What are you talking about?" Bree said hotly. "Karen would never— Ouch!"

It hadn't been a tap on the foot this time but a swift kick in the ankle.

"If your attorney is reputable," Gianni said, "and I am sure that he is, he'll tell you that proving undue influence will involve a lengthy and expensive court battle."

"Perhaps." The *signora* lifted her cup to her lips. "Neither is a problem, *signore.* Expense will not be an issue, and the time remaining to me will be sufficient for my needs."

"You mean," Gianni said, "you know you're going to lose and you only want to delay things as long as possible."

The old woman gave him a little smile.

Gianni pushed his coffee aside. "*Signora.* We have no wish to deny you contact with Lucia. We'll be happy to bring her to see you often."

"That's an interesting but useless offer. It does not address the problem of raising Lucia. Even if Tomasso were still alive, such visits would be pleasant but not meaningful. For one thing, occasional visits have little impact on a child's development. For another, involvement with children is a joy for some women. It never was for me. I had a son because it was expected of me, not because of any deep maternal yearnings."

"My God," Bree said. "Gianni? Did you hear that?"

"Then why would you even want to be involved in raising a child again?" Gianni said, ignoring Briana.

"Nurses, nannies, governesses... They are the ones who will be involved. I need simply to pay their salaries."

"Then," Gianni said, struggling to keep his temper, "putting all those things aside, do you really want to spend the next months, even years, in courtrooms?"

"Gianni," Bree said, "you can't let her—"

"All that time," he said tightly, "all that publicity. Will it be good for the Massini name, do you think?"

The *signora's* lips thinned. "You threatened me with that earlier, *Signore* Firelli, and I admit it does not please me, but my grandson left me no choice."

"No choice than to spend a fortune in legal fees, drag your name and the child's through the tabloids and, in the end, lose?" Gianni sat forward. "You *will* lose. You must know that. Have you discussed this with your attorney? I'm sure he'll tell you the same thing, *signora.* A last will and testament is a binding document, especially when it concerns the welfare of a child. Courts always prefer to follow the wishes of the parents."

Did he see the cup tremble, ever so slightly, in the *signora's* hand?

"Do you want your great-grandchild to grow up as an item in the tabloid press? Tomasso and Karen wanted us to raise Lucia, to give her the love and care they would have given her, not to see the Massini name and their daughter's life chronicled in sleaze sheets around the world."

Oh, yes. The cup was definitely trembling. The *signora* knew she was heading for thin ice.

"You make an excellent case, *signore*. Unfortunately you've left something out."

"And that is?"

The thin lips curled with contempt.

"Morality. Propriety. Decency." She put the cup on the saucer with enough force to make it shudder. "I am aware such things have little bearing in today's world, but they are important in mine."

Bree rolled her eyes. "Lovely. She's prepared to ignore Tommy's and Karen's wishes, to let the baby be fodder for the tabloids, and she has the nerve to talk about—"

"Bree." Gianni smiled, though smiling was the last thing he felt like doing. They were close to settling this; instinct, honed by years in the courtroom, told him so, but Briana could ruin it if she let anger get the best of her.

He pushed back his chair and walked around the table to where she sat.

"Bree," he said, his voice soft but his hands hard as he laid them on her shoulders, "Let *Signora* Massini speak."

"You have been blunt, *Signore* Firelli. I shall be blunt, as well. You are correct. My actions will do little but delay things."

"Then why—"

Gianni pressed down on Bree's shoulders. She huffed but fell silent.

"My attorney and his firm are clever. They will, as you

said, see to it that determining guardianship of Lucia will take years. Many years.'' The thin mouth curved again, this time in a self-satisfied smile. "By the time you gain full legal possession of her, she will be old enough to have been taught a proper moral code. She will not be affected by living in a house with a man and woman who have chosen to live together in sin.''

The *signora's* voice had risen on the final words so that they seemed to hang in the silence of the huge room.

Then Briana laughed.

"Are you serious?" She peered up at Gianni, standing motionless and stone-faced behind her. "Is she serious? She's going to keep that little girl here because she thinks you and I are sleeping together and she doesn't approve?''

"She is serious," Gianni said softly.

Signora Massini plucked her cane from where it hung on the arm of her chair and stamped it against the marble floor. As if by magic, the butler hurried into the room.

"Indeed, I am quite serious. And now, if you will excuse me, it is getting late. Bartolemo, help me to my—''

Gianni cleared his throat. *"Signora."*

Tomasso's grandmother gave a put-upon sigh. "What is it now? You have nothing to say that I wish to hear.''

"On the contrary," Gianni said quietly. His hands cupped Bree's shoulders. She looked up, saw a glitter in his eyes that made her belly knot. "We could have saved ourselves this entire discussion, *signora.''* He took a deep breath. "You see, just this afternoon, Miss O'Connell did me the honor of agreeing to become my wife.''

CHAPTER TEN

SOMEHOW, Bree got through the next few minutes without saying a word.

Somehow?

She gave an unladylike snort as Gianni propelled her through the door into their bedroom.

The combination of his hands digging into her shoulders and her shock at what he'd said had proven to be an effective gag, but the second the door shut behind them, she jerked away from him and exploded.

"Are you crazy? Telling that woman I'd agreed to...that I'd said I would..." She flung her arms wide. "I can't even say it! My God, Firelli, what came over you?"

"Calm down."

"Calm down? Calm down?" Bree's voice rose to new heights as she kicked off one shoe and watched with satisfaction as it bounced off the wall. "Do you think she's stupid? Do you think she'll really fall for that? Do you think—"

"Damn it," Gianni growled, "lower your voice! She'll hear you."

"She'll hear me?" Bree repeated incredulously. "You think she won't see through that incredible lie?"

"Did you hear her response, or were you too busy working up to hysteria?"

"I heard it, all right. She said she was surprised. That her attorney had told her we hardly knew each other."

"And I said her attorney was wrong. That your brother-in-law, Tomasso and I had been friends when we were kids, and that you and I have been seeing each other for a long time."

"And you think she bought that?"

"It doesn't matter a damn if she did or if she didn't. The last thing she said is what counts."

Bree gave a snort even less ladylike than the first.

"You mean, that she's delighted to know Lucia will be raised in a moral household? That now she can be assured the baby's upbringing will not sully the Massini name?"

"Exactly." Gianni stalked to the window, turned and stalked back again. "That's all that matters to her."

"Big surprise." Bree sent her second shoe flying. "But there's one little problem, Firelli. We are *not* getting married. It doesn't matter if she hears me now or not. She'll figure it out soon enough. And here I always thought a person needed a functioning brain to get through law school. Boy, was I wrong!"

Gianni glared at Briana. Wonderful. Dinner with the Wicked Witch and now a crazy woman for dessert. Hadn't he spotted a drinks tray somewhere in this room? The damned place was so big you needed a road map.

Yes. There it was, on the sideboard. Two decanters and a couple of glasses. He had no idea what the decanters held. One liquid was amber, one was a pale gold.

He didn't care.

What he needed was a drink. The sharp burn of alcohol to clear his head and then maybe, just maybe, he could get back the clarity of that one moment when telling the *signora* that he and Bree were getting married had seemed the solution to their problem.

How could he have imagined that?

Bree was still raving, pacing back and forth, throwing up her hands, telling him that he'd succeeded in making things more complicated.

"It's your specialty," she said. "Complicating things."

Was she referring to his ploy to get the baby, or to what had happened a few hours before, in this bed? Gianni opened one of the decanters, poured an inch of its contents into a heavy crystal glass and tossed it back.

Scotch. Good scotch that went down like warm velvet. He poured another.

Yes. She had to be talking about that. About him making love to her. Why go back to that? It was over. It hadn't meant a thing. He couldn't even remember what it had been like, tasting her mouth. Her breasts. Feeling her nipples on his tongue, her heat burning against his hand. Hearing her soft cries, watching her beautiful face as she came for him. For him. Only for…

Jesus.

He slammed down the glass. He needed a clear head, not another shot of whisky.

"Enough," he said.

"I haven't even gotten started! How could you? What were you thinking? Why on earth would you say—"

"Enough," he roared, and slammed his fist down on the sideboard. The tray jumped. So did Bree, he noted with grim satisfaction. "Sit down and listen."

"Listen to what? I can't think of anything you could say that would—"

"Let me talk."

"I already did that, and where did it get us?" Bree blew a curl off her forehead and folded her arms. "In a mess," she said, answering her own question, "that's where."

"Telling the *signora* we were getting married was—it was expedient."

"You mean, it was dumb."

"If you'd stop raving and start thinking, you'd see it."

"What I saw was her face. She may have sounded as if she bought the story but one look said otherwise."

"I admit, she looked…skeptical."

"Skeptical?" Bree barked out a laugh. "That's a nice way of putting it."

Gianni felt a muscle knot in his jaw. She was right. *Signora* Massini had looked as if she'd just watched a magician try to convince an audience he was going to conjure a rabbit from a hat when they could already see its ears peeking above the crown.

"Then we'll just have to make her believe it," he said, folding his arms. "Or don't you want us to raise Lucia?"

"The law is on our side. You told me that a dozen times."

"It is." He paused. "But the *signora's* right. The law can move slowly."

"Tomasso and Karen left a will."

"For God's sake," he snapped, "use your head! She laid it out for us. For starters, we're on her turf."

"So? The will—"

"Bree, damn it, keep quiet for once and pay attention!" Gianni ran a hand through his hair, paced away from her, then paced back. Bree was right. He *had* told her the law was with them—and then he'd come face to face with the *signora.* Trying to explain his grandmother, Tomasso had once called her the original immovable object.

Tommy, Gianni thought with a sigh, *paisano, you were right.*

"Well, we have a couple of choices," he said, tucking his hands in his pockets. "One, we kidnap Lucia."

"That's fine with me."

"And we get stopped in Palermo—assuming we get that far—and spend the next hundred years in jail."

"Don't yell, okay? I just have to point out that the will is legal."

"Kidnapping isn't."

Much as she hated to admit it, he had a point. Bree sighed

and rubbed her forehead, where a permanent ache seemed to have taken up residence.

"You said we had a couple of options."

"We can dig in our heels for a legal battle. I'll contact some people I know, ask them to recommend someone here, the lawyers will meet, face off…" Gianni shook his head. "And maybe, with luck, Lucia will come to live with us by the time she's ready to start school."

"Are you serious?"

"They can stall us with endless delaying tactics. That's a given in any court system. And we're dealing with a powerful woman. Who knows how many buttons she can push?"

"What about our consulate? Won't it help us?"

"Help us do what? Intervene in what's basically a custody fight?" Gianni shook his head. "The government's not going to get involved in this, Bree."

Bree stared at him. "Do you mean—she'll win?"

Gianni squatted in front of her. "She can only win if we give up, and we aren't going to do that. Tomasso asked this one last thing of me. I will honor his wish."

Bree's eyes searched Gianni's. That last statement had calmed her. She knew he meant it. She'd learned a lot about this man in an amazingly short period of time. He was, absolutely, a man of his word.

"And I'll honor Karen's," she said quietly.

"Then we're agreed. We have to do whatever it takes."

"And you really think going through the courts might take months?"

"Years," he said bluntly.

He took her hands in his. Her skin was cold; the fire had gone out of her eyes and been replaced by despair. He wanted to tug her into his arms, kiss her until her skin took on heat and color, until her eyes glittered with life, but that would only complicate things.

"Oh, God." She put her hand to her mouth. "Then, that beautiful little girl might end up in this awful place for a long time!"

His hands tightened on hers. "She might—but we're not going to let that happen."

Bree swallowed hard. "You think—you honestly think—*Signora* Massini will back off if she thinks we're getting married?"

"Yes."

"Gianni. You saw the expression on her face. She didn't believe you."

He knew she was right. He could still see the look the old woman had given him, hear the cynicism in her voice when she said, "Really. How nice for you both." What sense was there in denying it?

"Okay." He gave a rueful smile. "Maybe not."

Bree touched her hand to his cheek. "You're a good man, Gianni Firelli," she said softly. "Coming up with such an idea, even if it isn't going to work."

Gianni caught her hand again and held it in both of his.

"It can work, *cara.*"

"How? Tomasso's grandmother is a lot of things but she isn't stupid. What are we going to do, huh? Promise to send her an invitation to the wedding? She'll never release the baby on those terms."

"You're right, she won't." He lifted her hand to his lips, spread her fingers and pressed a kiss to her palm. "Still there's a way."

"What way?"

"You won't like it."

"Is it legal?"

He nodded.

"That's good."

"Better still, it's guaranteed to work."

"If it works and it's legal, what won't I like?" She smiled. "Come on, tell me."

His eyes caught hers. In the sudden silence, Bree could hear the thunder of her heart.

"We get married," Gianni said.

AN HOUR LATER, they were seated facing each other on opposite sides of the bed. Bree was still shaking her head and saying no, no, they couldn't.

They could, Gianni insisted, of course they could. This was nothing more than a gambit in a chess game where the queen was an intractable old woman.

"I am not going to marry you," Bree said. "The *signora* will know it's only so we can get Lucia from her."

"She won't. I'll talk to her, explain that we'd decided, on our way here, that we wanted to make our relationship legal—"

"We don't have a relationship!"

"—and that we intended to keep that decision private," Gianni continued, as if she hadn't spoken, "but that we changed our minds when we realized her concerns are about Lucia."

"She has no concerns about Lucia," Bree said hotly. "Her only 'concerns' are for herself."

"I know that. You know that. But there's no reason we can't let her think we see her point."

Bree shook her head. "She won't believe you."

Gianni gritted his teeth. "Why are you so damned stubborn? All right. Let's try it your way. Suppose she doesn't believe me. So what?"

"What do you mean, so what? If she realizes we're only getting married to placate her, she'll—she'll—"

"She'll what? Tell us the marriage isn't to her liking? Listen to me, Bree. People everywhere marry for all kinds of reasons. In a place like this, an old-world culture, it's even more true. Marriages in these hill towns are often based on things that have nothing to do with love.''

Nothing to do with love.

Bree knew he was right. People did marry for reason that had nothing to do with love, and love would surely have no bearing on this marriage—assuming she were fool ish enough to agree to it. Then, why did his blunt word hurt so much?

''Bree. You know I'm right. Men and women marry for money. For property. For the good of their families. Tha we would marry for the benefit of a child would be a pos itive thing in the *signora's* eyes.''

''But not in mine. I've always thought—I'd imagine marrying a man I felt—I felt something for.''

Gianni reached for her hands. ''You felt something thi afternoon,'' he said, his eyes on hers.

Color rushed to her face. ''That was sex.''

''Sex is a part of marriage. An important part.''

''No.'' Bree tore her hands from his and got to her feel ''I can't do it.''

''Can't, or won't?'' His voice hardened as he rose from the bed. ''There's a difference.''

''Gianni, try to understand. This is—it's wrong.''

''Indeed,'' he said with sudden coldness. ''And letting this woman, the last person in the world Tomasso and Karen would have chosen to be Lucia's guardian, letting her raise their daughter is right?''

''Of course it isn't! But—''

Bree's words stumbled to a halt. But what? Tomasso' grandmother had made it clear her only concern was for propriety. One lie, and propriety was no longer a problem

The baby would be theirs.

Gianni must have read something in her face. He came to her and clasped her shoulders. His touch was light, his voice a whisper.

"We have no choice, Bree. We have to do this for Tomasso. For Karen. For the baby."

She looked up at him. "If—if we did this, how soon would we—"

"As soon as Italian law permits. With luck, you'd be my wife before the week ends."

His wife. She would be Gianni's wife. Bree began to tremble. "I don't—I can't imagine—I just can't—"

"I can," he said, and kissed her.

The kiss was soft as a butterfly's wing, only the brush of his mouth on hers. Bree made a little sound and leaned toward him; Gianni groaned, his arms swept around her and gathered her, hard, against him.

And she was lost.

She was a creature born on the sigh of the wind and Gianni was her world, her safe haven, he was—he was—

With a soft cry of alarm, she tore free of his embrace. "Don't," she whispered. "I can't think when you—when you—"

"Don't think," he said fiercely. "Just say yes."

Funny, but she'd seen a hundred movies with scenes like this. The man and woman standing close together, he gazing down at her, asking her the question she'd been longing to hear...

Except, this wasn't a movie.

Briana felt a sudden ache in her heart. She was close to weeping and couldn't imagine the reason. Gianni's question was all business.

Her answer would be the same.

"If I agree," she said, "it will only be on certain conditions."

"Name them."

"It won't be a real marriage."

A tight smile tilted across his mouth. "You're the one who keeps reminding me that the *signora* isn't a stupid woman. Have you changed your mind, *cara?* Do you suddenly think we've only to go away for a day, come back and tell her we're now husband and wife and she'll fall for it?''

''No.'' Bree took a shuddering breath. ''No,'' she said carefully, ''I know she'd never buy a story like that.''

''Then, what are you suggesting?''

Another deep breath. Suddenly she couldn't seem to get enough air into her lungs.

''We marry, as you suggested. We take the baby. We go back to the States—and we get a divorce.''

His eyes went flat. ''I see.''

''It's the only way to handle this,'' she said quickly. ''The marriage will satisfy the *signora.*''

''And the divorce will satisfy you.''

''You, too.'' Her throat felt parched and she swallowed convulsively. ''I mean—I mean, you don't want to marry me any more than I want to marry you. Right?''

The muscle in his cheek knotted and unknotted. ''Absolutely right.''

''You said this was an old-world culture. Well, what we need is an old-world marriage of convenience.''

''And a quick dissolution of it.''

''Exactly. That suits you, doesn't it?''

There was a long silence. Then he shrugged. ''Why not?''

''Good.'' Bree ran the tip of her tongue over her bottom lip. ''There's just one other thing…''

A tight smile lifted one corner of his mouth. ''What more could there be, *cara,* after we've said 'yes' to a quick marriage and a quicker divorce?''

''Another condition.''

''What?''

She hesitated. Gianni could see her working up to something and he knew, instinctively, he wouldn't like it but then, he hadn't liked the initial condition either, and wasn't that crazy? If she hadn't suggested the divorce, he would have.

This marriage was about expediency. It had to do with honoring Tomasso's memory and nothing else.

"What other condition?"

"This will be a marriage in name only."

"A marriage in…" His eyes narrowed. "What in hell is that supposed to mean?"

Bree could feel her pulse beating high and fast in her throat.

"We're not going to do—what we did this afternoon." Gianni arched one eyebrow and she felt her face heating. "Don't look at me as if you don't remember."

"Believe me, *cara,* I remember exactly what we did this afternoon. And the reason is…?"

"It's wrong."

His eyes darkened. "We're both adults. We're attracted to each other. Why should making love be wrong?"

"Because it is. Because it complicates things. I told you that before."

"When you said that, we were unsure of what lay ahead. Now we know. We've seen the baby and why Tomasso's grandmother objects to giving her to us." Gianni took a step closer and cupped her face. "We've even figured out how to make that objection go away. How can we complicate this by making love?"

"We're Lucia's guardians, Gianni. That responsibility will be with us for a very long time. It's like a—a partnership."

"So?"

"So, would you sleep with your business partner?"

"If you'd seen any of the partners in the law firm I belonged to, *cara,* you wouldn't ask that question."

"I'm not going to debate this. Those are my terms. No sex."

Gianni frowned. Damned if she wasn't right. You didn't sleep with business associates, not if you wanted to be able to continue the business relationship after you grew tired of each other—and you always grew tired of each other. That was the way it was with men and women.

But they'd already violated that policy. They'd made love and, damn it, he wanted more of her. She wanted more of him, too. He knew it. The way she'd moaned in his arms today, the way she'd trembled. The scent of her, the silkiness of her skin...

"No sex," she said, her voice trembling just a little. She cleared her throat. "We won't sleep together, Gianni. If you want me to say yes to this marriage, you'll say yes to that."

His eyes weren't just dark, they were storm clouds.

"Let me get this straight. I give you my name. In return, I get an empty bed and a fast divorce. Have I got that right?"

"Oh, that's charming. You're going to *give* me your name?" Bree tossed her head. Why had she been so nervous a minute ago? How could she have forgotten this man's impossible ego? "Get this straight, *signore*. The only thing you're *giving* me is a temporary marriage I don't want."

"Stop wagging your finger at me."

"We're doing this for our friends. For their daughter. Not so you can have me in your bed."

"I told you to stop shaking your finger at me, Briana."

"And I'm telling you, take it or leave it. We do this my way, or... What are you doing? Let go of me, damn it! Firelli. Firelli—"

His arms folded around her and his mouth took hers in a long, almost savage kiss. Bree fought. Bree struggled. And then she let it happen, let the taste of him flood through her, let the feel of him heat her blood. She whispered his name, wound her arms around his neck as he slid his hands down her back, cupped her bottom and lifted her into him until their bodies were melded together.

His hand came up, cupped her breast. She groaned into his mouth as his fingers played over her nipple, as he slid his hand under her skirt, caressed her thigh, moved closer and closer to her feminine core...

And then he thrust her from him.

"The first rule of negotiation," he said curtly. "Don't demand terms you're not prepared to follow."

Bree launched herself at him. "Bastard," she hissed. "No good, slimy, good-for-nothing—"

Her hand flew toward his face. Gianni caught it and forced her arm behind her back.

"Watch what you say to me, *cara*. Watch what you do. Deep down, I'm still Sicilian. I don't take insults lightly."

He let her go and she fell back against the wall, hot with rage, shaking with it...

Stuck with it.

There wasn't a thing she could do that would make her feel better. She couldn't hit him, couldn't storm out of the room, couldn't even tell him to take his sorry self and sleep elsewhere because he'd beaten her to it.

As she watched, he flung a pillow and blanket on the chair that stood farthest from the bed.

"The bed is yours," he growled. "And if you say one more word to me tonight, I promise, you'll regret it."

"What I regret," Bree shrieked, "is that I ever had the misfortune to meet you!"

But she didn't say it until after he'd gone into the bathroom and slammed the door.

GIANNI GLOWERED at his reflection in the mirror.

He looked like a man who wanted to wander into a bar, pick a fight with the meanest looking SOB in the place and work off his frustrations with his fists. If he'd been anywhere but here, in the forgotten middle of nowhere, that was exactly what he'd have done.

Grumbling under his breath, he turned on the cold water and splashed some over his face.

He could get into the Ferrari and drive for a while. The *signora* would probably hear him leave the house but what did that matter? The walls of this old crypt were God only knew how many feet thick. Still, the way he and Bree had been going at it, the old witch had surely heard them by now.

The real problem with taking the car was that Bree would undoubtedly lock him out. He'd have to kick the door in when he got back, which wasn't a bad idea because then he'd swing her into his arms, carry her to that damned bed, kiss her mercilessly until she—until she—

Gianni groaned, grasped the edge of the sink and closed his eyes.

He wasn't a man who started fights with strangers. He wouldn't force himself on a woman…except, damn it, that was the whole point.

That was why he was so furious.

They both knew he wouldn't have to force himself on Briana.

She'd come to him willingly. Eagerly. She'd open her mouth for the touch of his tongue, part her thighs so he could lie between them. And when he entered her, he'd do it slowly. So slowly. Moving inside her. Feeling the kiss of her wet heat.

Gianni stared into the mirror again. The man that looked back might have been a stranger.

Complications? He wanted to laugh. That was too simple a word. He was in over his head, joined to a spitfire first by the guardianship of a child and soon by the bonds of matrimony.

So she wouldn't sleep with him. So what? He wasn't an

animal in rut. They'd have to suffer through a sham of a marriage for, what? A week? They'd marry, fly home, and married life would be history.

Just thinking about how simple it was made him feel better.

The water was still running. He ducked his head under it until his teeth chattered. Now, he could go back into that room and behave like a civilized man. He'd even apologize to Briana for losing his temper.

Except, she was asleep.

Gianni shut off the light, fought his way into a chair that wouldn't have held a poodle, let alone a man, and managed to get a couple of hours of sleep.

He woke just after dawn, body aching as if he'd been drawn on a rack, but still with that good feeling of being in control of his emotions. He went downstairs, found the kitchen and the coffee, then closeted himself in the library for a two-hour session on his cell phone.

Now he'd wait for Bree to wake up. Then he'd tell her what he'd arranged, apologize for going crazy last night, assure her he had no problem at all with her no-sex condition.

Gianni opened the door and slipped into the bedroom.

She was lying on her side. Like him, she'd slept in her clothes. Her hair was spread over the pillow; her lips were rosy and slightly parted. Her skirt was rucked up to her thighs.

She had such long legs. He could remember the feel of them, locked around his waist. So what? He was still in control, still going to make that apology.

"Bree," he said softly, and when she opened her eyes and looked at him, he told her that they'd be married by nightfall.

Her pupils dilated with shock. "By nightfall?"

"Yes." He was pleased with how calm he sounded. "The sooner the better. I had to pull some strings, but it's all set."

She sat up against the pillows, lifted her arms and pushed her hair back from her face. His gaze fell to her breasts. He could still remember their taste. The taste of her mouth.

"Married. You. And me."

"Yes. And there's something else, something I should have said last night."

The words *I'm sorry* were on the tip of his tongue. God, she was so beautiful. So much a woman.

"What should you have said?"

Still calm, still in control, he said he'd been thinking about that second condition.

"And?" she said, her eyes locked to his.

Gianni took a breath. "And," he heard himself say, "I'll be patient. I'll wait until you come to your senses, *cara*." His voice roughened. "And when you do, I'll take you into my bed."

CHAPTER ELEVEN

ONE NIGHT on Italian soil and Gianni Firelli had turned into an arrogant, dyed-in-the-wool Sicilian. Fortunately he was so smugly, disgustingly self-centered that it was almost painfully easy to outthink him.

She'd been so angry when he'd delivered what amounted to a challenge that she hadn't been able to think straight. Hours went by before she calmed down enough to realize how to handle his statement.

She'd simply ignore it.

He knew she wouldn't turn her back on the baby. She'd go through with the marriage. After that, Gianni could wait for her to go to his bed until the cows came home.

She didn't even bother responding. Instead she stalked past him, head high, went into the bathroom and slammed the door even harder than he had the prior night.

He was gone when she came back into the bedroom and she managed to avoid him all morning, but at noon she walked into the library without realizing he was there, talking on his cell phone. She turned on her heel and walked straight out again, but not before overhearing part of a conversation.

"Yes," she heard him say, "that's right. The flight is scheduled for eight this evening."

He was arranging their trip home. They wouldn't have to wait to start divorce proceedings. Goodbye, Italy. Hello, America. Soon, she could tell her husband-of-convenience to go to hell.

What a lovely moment that would be!

That thought kept her smiling during the long day. So did the baby, who loved having her belly kissed. Then Gianni came into the garden where she sat on the grass with Lucia in her lap and announced that she had an hour left.

She knew what he meant. An hour until she became his wife. She felt a rush of panic but she'd sooner have died than let him know it.

"An hour until what?" she said sweetly, and then she rounded her eyes. "Oh, of course. Until we get married. Sorry. I almost forgot."

He didn't smile back. He looked hard and grim and altogether forbidding. He also looked as beautiful as she'd ever seen him, in a dark suit and white silk T-shirt, his hair damp from the shower and curling lightly as it fell over his forehead.

Legions of women would have given their souls for this moment, but she wasn't one of them. She wasn't a fool. She knew what he wanted of her—not just sex but the passion that would turn her pathetic and defenseless, that would leave her heartbroken when this joke of a marriage ended.

"I'll be ready," she said in a cool voice. "Don't worry about it."

He did smile, then, in a way that made her breath catch. "I'm not worrying about a thing, *cara,*" he said softly.

As he strolled away, she handed the baby to the nurse and concentrated on the fact that they'd be on that plane before the ink was dry on their marriage license.

THEY WERE MARRIED at Trapani, in a wedding hall set aside for civil ceremonies. She'd expected a dank town office manned by a bored clerk but the hall was handsome and the mayor was charming. He took her hand and kissed it and spoke to her in Italian. The translator, a legal requirement for non-Italian couples entering into marriage, beamed and told her the mayor thought she was the most beautiful bride he'd ever seen and that he wished her much happiness.

Caught off-guard, Bree felt the prick of tears. The mayor undoubtedly told all the brides they were beautiful. It was what he'd said about happiness that got to her. A woman should be happy on her wedding day. She should be happy, assuming she wanted a wedding day in the first place.

Bree had never given it much thought. If she had, she surely wouldn't have dreamed of marrying a man like the one standing next to her. None of this was real, of course, but if it were, if Gianni loved her, he'd want more than her love in return. He'd want everything. Her heart, her mind, her very essence.

Nobody was ever going to lay that kind of claim to her.

The ceremony was mercifully brief. When it was over, the *signora* shook hands with Gianni and even with her. The nurse wiped away her tears and offered a quick kiss on the cheek. The baby, lying in the nurse's arms, gurgled happily and waved her arms.

"I am pleased," the *signora* said.

The queen had given her blessing. It was the final stamp of approval. Bree felt a little of the tension drain away. She shot a surreptitious glance at her watch and felt even better.

In a little more than two hours, they'd be on that plane heading for the States. She decided to help move things along.

"Gianni," she purred, leaning delicately into him, "don't you think we ought to get started?"

He looked down at her as if she'd just performed some fabulous trick. "I know you want us to be alone, *cara*," he purred back, "but surely we can spare a few moments to chat with our guests."

Guests? The *signora* and the nurse were their witnesses, but Bree went along with the game. She slid her arm through his. Why not torture him, if only a little?

"I'm sure *Signora* Massini will understand, darling. You can always phone her from the plane."

Gianni smiled, and something in the smile made the hair rise on the back of her neck.

"What plane, *darling?*" he said.

"Why—why, the one that leaves Palermo at eight. The one going to New York."

"Ah. *That* plane." Gianni slipped his arm around her waist and drew her close against him. "Unfortunately it will take off without us."

Bree stared at him. "But I heard you. In the library. You were making reservations…"

"I was canceling the arrangements I'd made for a charter flight home." He smiled, but the smile never reached his eyes. "The *signora* suggested we not leave quite yet."

"The *signora* suggested?" Bree tried to pull away but Gianni's arm only tightened around her. "And, just like that, you gave in? You didn't think about asking me what I wanted to do?"

"We can think of these next few weeks as a honeymoon," he said easily.

She knew he was talking that way for the *signora's* sake but she didn't care. If anything, it only made her angrier. Did he really think this mockery of a marriage gave him the right to make unilateral decisions?

"I want to go home, Firelli. Now."

"You will do as you're told, Briana," he said without any semblance of a smile.

Bree blinked her eyes. The mayor, the translator, the *signora* and yes, even the nurse were all watching the little scene with interest but not with concern.

She was in a foreign country, without funds, without friends. She didn't even speak the language. For the first time, Briana realized how truly alone she was.

AN HOUR LATER, after Gianni had checked them into a suite in a hotel overlooking the sea, she turned on him in barely contained fury.

"You had the entire day to tell me about this," she said through her teeth.

Gianni sighed. They were standing on their terrace. He could imagine other couples on other terraces in this hotel that he'd been assured was the most romantic in all of Sicily, their arms around each other as they watched the sun kiss the bosom of the sea.

Why he'd thought he needed a romantic hotel was beyond him. This had never been anything but a sham marriage and now, to top things off, he had to listen to his pretend-bride rant and rage. He kept reminding himself that she was upset because they wouldn't be leaving Sicily just yet.

But, damn it, she didn't have to sound as if she'd just been sentenced to life in prison with a barbarian for a cellmate.

"I told you," he said grimly, "the *signora* sprang the news on me late this afternoon."

"That she wouldn't give us the baby until she was convinced we were really married."

"Yes."

"Of course we're married! What did she think that wedding was?"

"A trick. She saw right through us."

"I said she would, didn't I?"

Gianni narrowed his eyes. "If you're going to play the blame game, get your facts straight. What you said was that she'd see through our claim that we intended to get married."

"Your claim, Firelli. Not mine."

He thought about responding to that, then decided against it. Quarrelling with Briana was like playing a frenzied tennis match. Rally followed rally.

"She's agreed that she'll give the baby up at the end of the month."

"The end of...? That's three weeks away! What are we supposed to do in all that time?"

"I've rented a house."

Bree slapped her hands on her hips. "Does it ever occur to you to consult me on anything?"

"There wasn't time."

"No. I can see that. There wasn't time for anything except trying to force me into getting into bed with you!"

He moved fast, so fast that she stumbled and fell back against the wall. Gianni caught her wrist.

"At last," he growled as he towered over her, "something we can agree on. Wanting you in that bed was dead wrong."

"I'm glad to hear you ad—"

"I don't know what in hell I was thinking. A man wants a woman in his bed, not a shrew." He dropped her wrist and stepped back. "Don't wait up," he said coldly. "I won't be back until late."

Bree glared after him as he strode from the terrace. "My door will be locked. You just remember that!"

Gianni grabbed his jacket and slung it over his shoulder. "At least there's a couch in this damned place. I won't have to break my back in a chair made for dwarfs tonight."

"Did you hear me, Firelli? I said—"

He spun toward her, his hand on the doorknob. "I heard you," he said quietly. "Believe me, O'Connell, you don't have to worry. I have no intention of violating your precious 'condition' for marriage."

The door slammed shut after him. Bree stared at it and then, for no accountable reason, her eyes filled with tears.

"I'm delighted to hear it," she whispered. "Except—except my name isn't O'Connell anymore."

Then she leaned on the railing and wept.

THE NIGHT WAS THICK and black.

No moon. No stars. Not even a lamp to pierce the darkness of the hotel's parking lot. Stepping out of the Ferrari was like stepping into a pool of inky silence.

Gianni slipped into the hotel, walked through the vast lobby and nodded at the night clerk who looked surprised to see him. It was a good bet that this wasn't the kind of place where guests wandered around alone in the middle of the night.

The elevator took him to the top floor. Gianni went down the dimly lit hall to the suite, inserted his room key into the door and eased it open. The sitting room was pitch-black. He shut the door, then paused to let his eyes adjust to the dark.

The first thing he saw was the open bedroom door. His heart thudded. Bree would only have left it that way for a reason. She'd come to her senses. She was waiting for him, in the bed that should have been theirs...

Hell.

No way would that happen. He'd been lucky she wasn't waiting in the sitting room with a heavy object in her hand. A rock, maybe, he thought, and had to smile at the memory.

His smile faded. She'd only have left that door open for one reason. She'd left him. Called for a taxi, a private car... The point was, she was gone.

He tossed his jacket aside, hurried into the bedroom and switched on the light.

He was right. She was gone. The bed hadn't even been touched... But her suitcase, standing next to his near the closet, was still there.

His gut twisted into a knot. "Bree?" He went to the bathroom, opened the door...

Empty.

"Bree," he said again, "Briana?"

The terrace was empty, too. His gaze was drawn to the railing, to the sea beating far below.

No. God, no…

"Gianni?"

He swung toward the sitting room. The spill of light from the bedroom lent soft illumination to the couch and to the woman huddled on it.

"Bree."

He went to her quickly, angry words building in his throat, but when he saw her, he knew his anger was only a cover for a relief so profound it stunned him.

His wife was sitting in a corner of the couch. She wore one of the heavy silk robes provided by the hotel and her hair hung over her shoulders in a wild golden cloud. Her eyes, when she raised them to his, were swollen and red.

Possibilities danced through his head accompanied by a rage so profound he thought he might explode. Someone had broken in. Someone had hurt her.

Hurt his Briana.

Gianni squatted in front of her and took her icy hands in his.

"What happened?"

She looked down and shook her head.

"Damn it, tell me what happened! Did someone hurt you?"

Another shake of the head. He felt some of the weight lift from his heart.

"*Cara,*" he said more gently, "talk to me. Tell me why you're crying."

"I don't know," she whispered. "I don't know why I'm crying."

Bree knew it sounded stupid but that was the truth. Gianni had been gone for hours; she'd wept for almost all that time and she didn't know the reason.

Maybe it was because she'd thought about how crazy he

could be, driving the Ferrari, and pictured him dead on the road. Maybe it was because she'd imagined him sitting in a bar, smiling at a woman who was happy to smile back.

Or maybe it was because this was her wedding night, real or not, and because she'd spent every minute since they'd agreed to the ceremony lying to him and to herself, pretending she didn't want him to take her in his arms, to kiss her, to whisper to her and, yes, make love to her.

Gianni stroked the riot of curls back from her cheeks.

"Briana," he murmured, "*cara, mi dispiace.* I'm sorry."

She shook her head. "You have nothing to be sorry for. You were right. We had to go through with the wedding, and we have to stay on long enough to convince the *signora* this marriage is real."

"But I should have consulted you first. You were right, each time. I'm just not—I'm not used to sharing decisions." He cleared his throat. "And I should never have expected anything from you."

"Expected…" Smudges of color rose in her face. "Sex, you mean."

"Making love. That was what I wanted, Bree. For us to lie in each other's arms and finally make love." He cupped her face, his fingers weaving into her hair. "I would never expect you to humble yourself to me, *cara.* Despite my stupid words, you must know that."

Bree offered a wobbly smile. "I know."

"No matter how badly a man wants a woman, she must want him, too."

Another shaky smile. "Do you know, the longer we stay in Sicily, the more you sound like a Sicilian?"

He laughed softly. "That sound you hear isn't the sea, *cara,* it's a collective sigh of approval from all my ancestors."

There was a silence. Then she drew a deep breath. "If we're dealing in truths…"

"Yes?"

"Then—then, here's mine." Bree raised her head until their eyes met. "I wanted you as much as you wanted me." She paused. "I still do."

He felt his blood leap. "Are you sure?"

"Yes. Oh, yes, yes, yes—"

Gianni took her mouth in a long, deep kiss. She moaned softly as his tongue swept over hers. When she did, he rose to his feet, taking her with him. He could feel the heat, the softness of her body through the robe, and he gathered her close and kissed her again.

She sighed, rose to him, clasped his face between her hands and he felt his swiftly hardening arousal turn to stone.

Quickly his mouth hot on hers, he carried her into the bedroom. The lamp he'd lit when he was trying to find her cast a soft glow on the bed. He set her down beside it and kissed her eyes, her mouth, her throat. Her head fell back; her lashes drooped languorously to her cheeks and he felt her start to tremble.

"Gianni…"

"Yes, sweetheart. Yes, *cara.*" He took her hand, kissed it, then pressed it against his erection. "It's the same for me."

It was. God, it was. His body was on fire.

Slowly he told himself, *slowly.* In so many ways, this would be their very first time together.

He undid her sash, eased the robe back on her shoulders. She caught it as it began to slip away but he captured her hands, brought them to her sides and let the garment become a lake of silk at her feet.

She wore a bra and panties beneath it, but not the plain white cotton he remembered from the last time. This bra was sheer black silk; the thong that covered her mons was sheer black, too, and he felt a moment of crazed jealousy that it cupped her so intimately.

Slowly he bent his head to her breasts, kissed the barely contained flesh. "God, you're so beautiful," he whispered, and caught first one silk-covered nipple and then the other between his teeth.

Bree's cry rose into the night. He looked up, saw the expression on her face, the joy, the hunger, and he groaned and knew it was going to be difficult to keep himself under control. He wanted to tear off that thong, bury himself inside her...

No. Not yet. Not until he'd explored her.

He reached behind her, undid the bra, let it tumble to her feet. Her breasts were perfect, and waiting for the touch of his hands. His mouth. He cupped them, watched her face as he rolled the nipples between his fingers, savored the swift, telltale hiss of her breath and the way she sobbed his name.

Gianni ran his hand down her back, cupped her backside. His fingers drifted across her hip, beneath the thong. He could feel her heat. Her wetness.

He bent and eased the thong down her legs, steadied her with one hand while she stepped out of the wisp of silk. He lifted her foot to his mouth, kissed the arch. Then he stood up and cupped her shoulders. She made a woman's automatic gesture of modesty and he shook his head, took her hands again and kissed the palms.

"I want to see you, *cara*," he said hoarsely.

He took a step back and swept his eyes over her. She was exquisite. Perfect. Her face. Her breasts. The slender waist and curved hips, the long, elegant legs...

And she belonged to him.

To him, only to him. And, heaven help him, he had to have her now or lose what little remained of his sanity.

Gianni stripped off his clothes, took his bride in his arms and drew her down to the bed. At the first touch of his skin against hers, she arched against him and sighed his name. He took her mouth hungrily, nipped her throat, and suddenly he felt her hand on him. Holding him. Caressing him, her palm like velvet, her fingertips like silk along his swollen length.

"Bree," he said, "*cara,* be careful..."

"I don't want to be careful," she whispered.

The words inflamed him almost as much as her touch. He paused just long enough to reach back and dig into his trouser pocket for a small packet, tear it open with his teeth and slide the condom on.

Then he parted her thighs.

"Now," she said, "Gianni, please, please, please..."

Her words ended on a sob as he entered her. She was hot. Wet. Tight. So tight.

"Bree," he said, and caught her hands. "Briana."

She moved beneath him. Whispered his name. She moaned as he slid back, almost withdrawing from her, then thrust forward again.

He bent to her, inhaled the scent of vanilla and woman, kissed her mouth, her throat, her closed eyelids.

"Yes," she said, "Gianni, yes," and he groaned and thrust again, harder and harder while she wrapped her legs around him, and when she cried out and shuddered, Gianni threw his head back and let it happen, let the years of searching, of needing, of wanting something he'd never known fall away from him in a heart-stopping, explosive rush.

THEY FELL ASLEEP in each other's arms.

An hour later, an eternity later, they awoke and made love again. Before dawn, they stirred one last time. Gianni kissed his way down Bree's body, gently parted her thighs and tasted her sweetness with his tongue. She buried her hands in his hair, sobbed his name and when he sensed she was on the brink of that precipice that leads to the stars, he rose up, took her mouth with his, sank into her and they came together in a blur of heat and sighs.

Sometime during what little remained of the night, Gianni turned off the lamp and drew the blankets over them.

They slept on, entwined, until a knock at the door awakened them. "Who could that be?" Bree whispered.

"I'll take care of it." Gianni gave her a sweet, slow kiss. "First, though, good morning, *cara.*"

Whoever was at the door knocked again.

Bree smiled against his lips. "Don't answer," she said softly. "Whoever it is will go away."

Gianni grinned. "They'd better not. That's our breakfast and I can tell you right now, *signora,* I have one huge appetite."

She laughed softly. "You convinced me, *signore.* Get the door."

"Only if you promise not to move."

"I promise," she said, with such promptness that he knew she was lying. Smiling, he kissed the tip of her nose.

"You move from this bed, you'll have to pay the penalty."

"Mmm," she said, so sexily that Gianni almost decided answering the door wasn't worth it. But her stomach chose that moment to give an unladylike growl and he chuckled, pulled on his trousers and went to admit the waiter.

Bree sprang from the bed, pulled on the robe and dashed into the bathroom. She used the toilet, brushed her teeth, ran her hands through her tangled hair and took a look in the mirror.

It was supposed to be a quick look, but how could it be when the woman smiling back at her was a stranger? Her eyes shone. Her skin glowed. Her mouth was pink and gently swollen but most of all, most of all, that woman in the mirror looked happy.

She looked ecstatic. She looked, she felt, like a woman who was in—who was in—

"Aha," Gianni said, wrapping his arms around her. "Thought you'd get away from me, did you?"

She turned in his embrace. Even the sound of his voice made her feel happy. An emotion far stronger, far more dangerous than desire quickened her heartbeat.

"Bree? What is it?"

She shook her head. For a minute, speech was impossible.

His smile faded. "Tell me what's wrong." He stroked the curls back from her temple. "Are you sorry about last night?"

"No. Oh, no. It was—it was wonderful."

Gianni's eyes darkened. "Yes," he said softly, parting the robe, cupping her breasts and teasing the tips with light brushes of his fingers, "yes, it was." Bree whispered his name, her voice breaking as she did, and he lifted her onto the edge of the vanity and stepped between her thighs. "*You* were wonderful," he said, and kissed her.

"Gianni?" Bree took a breath. "I want you to know I've never... What happened last night was..."

"For me, too," he said gruffly.

"I loved last night. Everything we did. I love—I love—"

She fell silent, stunned at what she'd almost said.

Gianni ran his hand down her belly. "What do you love, *cara?* Tell me."

Bree looked into his eyes. They were so green. So deep. If she weren't careful, she could fall into their depths and lose herself forever.

"Making love," she said quickly, "with you."

He nodded. She loved making love with him. That was good. It was what he'd wanted to hear. It was all he wanted to hear...

Wasn't it?

Wasn't it? he thought again, and because he suddenly felt as if he were balanced on a tightrope over the Grand Canyon, he blanked his mind by taking his wife in his arms and losing himself deep inside her.

CHAPTER TWELVE

THE HOUSE Gianni had rented was perfect.

It sat on a cliff overlooking the sea, bathed in sunlight and surrounded by flowers. An infinity pool in the lush gardens behind it seemed to meet the horizon and drop off the edge of the earth.

Gianni watched Briana as they walked through the bright, airy rooms. He'd made the rental arrangements sight unseen. The realtor had assured him the house was handsome and that had seemed enough.

Now, he wanted it to be beautiful for his wife's sake.

"What do you think?" he finally said, doing his best to sound casual.

Bree smiled at him. "It's beautiful."

He hadn't realized he'd been holding his breath until she said exactly what he'd been hoping to hear.

"Good." He gave a little laugh. "Terrific," he said, and slipped his arms around her.

"What about you? Do you like it, too?"

"If you're happy, I'm happy, *cara*," he said softly and as he kissed her, he knew he'd never said anything more true.

HAPPY?

After three more weeks, Bree knew there had to be a better word to describe what she felt. She was filled with joy. With ecstasy. She'd stepped into a new world. Who'd have dreamed it was what she'd wanted, what she'd searched for, all her life?

Sitting in the garden behind the house, watching Gianni play with the baby, her heart felt full to overflowing. She had a child she loved and a man she adored…

And a marriage that was a lie.

What had become of her uncomplicated life?

Marriage, love, babies…all those things had been for other women, not her. At least, this kind of love hadn't been for her. She'd told Fallon the truth all those weeks ago. The man for her would be easygoing. Uncomplicated.

Safe.

No ups, no downs. Their relationship would be predictable, a ship sailing a steady course on a smooth sea.

Then Gianni stormed into her life. There was nothing safe about him.

He was demanding. He had a temper. He made decisions without consulting her and when they made love, he wouldn't let her stay on the shore, where it was safe. He carried her out on the waves with him, took her up and up and up…

Briana's chest tightened.

She loved him so much that sometimes, after they made love, she wept. Who'd have dreamed you could love a man so fiercely that being with him could make you weep?

She never let him know any of that, of course. He was a good, caring man and he wanted her in his bed. He'd been honest about that from the beginning, even while she'd lied to him, to herself, about wanting him.

There'd been times since then when she'd thought—when she'd hoped—what he felt for her was more than desire. The way he talked to her. The looks he gave her. The easy touch of his hand over her hair as he walked by.

Surely all those things meant something.

Bree smiled as she watched him pretend to eat the baby's tiny toes.

The other night, at dinner, she'd looked up and found him watching her with something in his eyes that made her heart stop. *Ask him,* she'd thought. *Ask him what he feels for you.*

She hadn't. How could she? She'd always thought of herself as a courageous woman but it would take more than guts to ask such a question. What if you got the wrong answer?

She couldn't risk it. She'd lost her heart, but not her mind.

Still, she'd come awfully close last night. After they'd made love, while he was kissing her, he'd tasted her tears.

"Cara?" he'd said, "what is it? Why are you crying?"

I'm crying because I love you and I don't want to lose you, she'd almost said. The admission had been a whisper away but just then Lucia began to cry. It was time for her bottle and it was Gemma's day off.

Bree had leaped from the bed like a woman with a reprieve in sight. Gianni had caught hold of her hand.

"You stay here," he'd said. "I'll take care of the baby."

"No," she'd said brightly, "that's okay. I'm already up."

She'd heated a bottle of formula, gone to the nursery, taken the baby in her arms and sat in a rocker, feeding her, crooning to her, wishing she'd been brave enough to tell Gianni the truth and glad she hadn't.

They had an arrangement, and he had not suggested changing it. One more week and they'd return to New York. She and Gianni would go through with a civilized divorce. She'd go back to being Briana O'Connell. He'd go back to being a bachelor. They'd live next door to each other, raise Lucia together, and she'd pretend she didn't care what happened on the other side of the wall that separated them any more than he did.

"Hey."

Bree looked up as Gianni sat down in the grass beside her, the baby in the curve of his arm. It was a hot day and he was wearing his swim trunks and nothing else. Lucia, wearing a diaper decorated with teddy bears, grinned toothlessly at the man she obviously adored.

You and me, kid, Bree thought, and her throat tightened.

"You okay?" Gianni said softly.

"Fine. Just enjoying the sun."

"Mmm." He leaned over and kissed her shoulder. "You taste delicious."

"Suntan lotion," she said, smiling. "How's Lucia doing? Does she need a diaper change?"

"I already did it."

His tone was smug. She could hardly blame him. Changing a diaper—a full diaper—had been a challenge. The first time she'd presented him with the job he'd stepped back in horror.

"Me?" he'd said.

"You," she'd replied. "We share everything, remember?"

"Yeah. Sure. But—" He'd wrinkled his elegant Roman nose. "*Cara.* The baby—the baby—"

"Smells," Bree had said blithely. "That's why her diaper needs changing."

To his credit, he'd done it. Oh, he'd gone a little pale but so had she the first couple of times. Truth was, she knew almost as little about babies as he did. Aunts gave bottles, changed wet diapers, not stinky ones and, in general, stood on the sidelines and made cheerful noises.

Being a mother was different.

No. She was a guardian. Not Lucia's mother. Not Gianni's wife. Not the woman he—

"There's that look again. Such deep thoughts, Briana."

Bree gathered her scattered thoughts. His smile was intimate; she felt her toes curl. Was there a more beautiful sight in the world than a gorgeous man holding a gorgeous baby?

"Not deep at all," she said lightly. "I was just wondering what we should have for lunch."

Gianni's smile tilted. His eyes got the dark, dangerous glint that made her breasts tingle.

"I know exactly what we should have," he said softly. "Come inside with me, *cara*."

"The baby…"

"It's her nap time." He got to his feet and held out his hand. "Come with me."

Briana let him lead her into the coolness of the house. He'd developed a way of giving orders that made them sound like wishes instead of commands, though she'd have followed his husky invitation to bed any time.

She drew the blinds in their bedroom while he took Lucia to the nursery, but she didn't undress. He liked to take off her clothes and she loved to have him do it. He came to her and took her in his arms. In the hushed afternoon darkness, he took her with him to a world she'd never imagined existed.

He might not love her, but he cared for her. No man could be this tender with a woman without caring.

I love you, she thought as he held her against him, *Gianni, I love you so much…*

Briana closed her eyes and tumbled into sleep.

SHE WAS ASLEEP.

Gianni touched his lips to Briana's hair. How he loved the smell of her. The taste. The feel of her in his arms.

The simple truth was, he loved her. If he didn't tell her soon, he was going to go crazy. He just had to find the right moment.

Be honest, Firelli.

There'd been a few right moments but he was a coward.

What if she looked at him after he'd opened his soul and said she didn't feel the same way?

Being so cautious was a new experience. All his life, he'd gone after what he wanted without hesitation. A scholarship to a university, when the other kids he knew—except for Tomasso and Stefano—were satisfied with high school diplomas. A degree in law, when most people in the old neighborhood thought their law was the only kind that mattered. A partnership in a firm where everybody's name but his was followed by Roman numerals, and then the move to the Federal Prosecutor's office when his law partners said he was insane to give up what he had.

Until now, he'd set his eye on the prize and gone after it.

This was different.

His ego had been on the line those other times. Now, it was something much more vulnerable.

His heart.

These had been the best three weeks of his life. Soon, they'd fly back to New York. He didn't want to; he'd thought about staying here longer but there was an important case waiting for him and he was obligated to try it.

He'd always been good about meeting obligations. He'd lost his father when he was nine; his mother, accustomed to an old-world role in her marriage, had been lost. Before long, he'd been making grown-up decisions. How to stretch the pitifully small social security payments to meet their bills. Who to pay first each month, the grocer, the butcher or the landlord?

At the beginning, he'd resented being the one in charge. After a while, it became second nature. He'd never realized that taking charge could also mean taking over...

Until Briana came along.

She sighed in her sleep and flung her arm across his chest. He drew her closer.

He'd denied her accusations at first but, deep down, he knew she was right. He didn't ask anyone's opinion, ever, he just made a decision and went with it.

That was okay when you were trying to fill your *papa's* shoes. Being hesitant, especially in the old neighborhood, would have been a sign of weakness. It was okay when you were a hotshot lawyer dealing with difficult clients, better than okay when you were taking down the sleaze of the earth in a federal courtroom.

But it made for problems when you fell in love with a tough-minded, independent woman.

That worried him, too. Not about spending his life with a woman who stood up to him. Hell, no. One thing he'd learned these three weeks was that a woman like that was just what he needed.

What troubled him was what Briana might think about him. What if she thought he was still too overbearing? What if he said, *Cara, I adore you and I won't divorce you,* and she said...

Whoa. He'd have to be careful. Forget, *I won't divorce you.* The way to say it was, *I don't want to divorce you.* Otherwise, they'd be right back where they'd started, glaring at each other, him telling her he didn't have to consult her on everything, her telling him he damned well had to.

He didn't want to risk losing her over words carelessly spoken.

Briana stirred in his arms. Her eyes opened and she smiled at him. "Did I fall asleep?"

Gianni nodded. "Yes. Right here, in my arms where you belong."

She got a strange look on her face. "Is that what you think? That I belong in your arms?"

Damn it, he'd done it again. Said something because he loved her that she'd probably heard as proof of his arrogance.

"*Cara.* I only meant—"

"I know what you meant."

He thought he'd ruined things with a misspoken phrase but she slipped on top of him, brought her open mouth to his, and they lost themselves in each other's arms.

THE DAYS SPED BY until there was only one night left.

Gemma had gone; they were alone in the house. Gianni, Briana, the baby—and a growing tension.

The atmosphere had taken a dark turn. Bree was edgy. So was Gianni. He knew the reason for his mood. He still hadn't found the right time, the right way to tell her he loved her.

As for Bree...he couldn't come up with a reason to explain her edginess. Last night, after dinner, he'd looked up and found her staring at him with something he couldn't read in her face.

"What's the matter, *cara?*" he'd said.

The muscles in her throat had constricted, as if she were swallowing hard.

"Nothing," she'd finally answered.

He'd known damned well she was lying but before he could pursue the topic, the baby started to wail.

Lucia, normally the most sunny of babies, had become fretful. They took her to a doctor who diagnosed an ear infection and assured them it was nothing to worry about. An antibiotic helped but she still woke up crying. They took turns walking the floor with her; when they weren't doing that, they were worrying. All in all, it made for little opportunity to have what Gianni had begun thinking of as A Serious Discussion.

This last night, he was a wreck. The baby, thank God, was fully recovered. He decided it was now or never. He had to tell his wife that he loved her and wanted her to stay married to him.

Gianni figured they'd go out for dinner. Maybe there'd be fewer distractions. They'd have to take the baby but he knew of a café in town with outdoor tables. There, over coffee, he could look into Briana's eyes and put the rest of his life in her hands.

But Bree didn't want to go out. She wanted to eat in. "I'll cook," she said. "After all, this is our last meal."

It was a portentous phrase. They looked at each other, both of them trying to smile.

"In this house, you mean," he said.

"Or anywhere, considering my talent in the kitchen."

He knew she was trying to diffuse the tension but why say something like that? Was she glad the month was at an end? Was she looking forward to going home, picking up the strands of her life, ending their marriage?

There was no point in negative thoughts. And perhaps staying home was a good idea. This way, they'd be alone. He'd wait until the baby was asleep. Then he'd take his wife in his arms or maybe go down on one knee, and tell her what was in his heart.

Sure, they were already married but this would be a real proposal. A declaration of love that would last forever…and he'd go crazy, if he had to wait until later.

Why not do it now?

"Briana," he said. "We have to talk."

He must have sounded urgent because she swung toward him, a strange expression on her face.

"About what?" she said, in such a choked voice he was suddenly afraid she knew what he was going to say and didn't want to hear it.

"*Cara.*" He held out his hand. "Come sit down. I want to tell—"

His cell phone rang. He almost groaned but he answered it, listened, then rolled his eyes. *La signora* was the last person he wanted to talk to right now.

She'd become an almost constant visitor this past week. She said she wanted to see the baby but she hardly looked at Lucia. Instead, each time she stopped by, her black eyes followed Briana's and Gianni's every move.

"*Signora*. Let me call you back…"

The *signora* interrupted him. Gianni sighed, listened…and smiled.

"What?" Bree mouthed, but he shook his head.

"Of course," he said. "Good. Very good. I appreciate it. I know, yes. You're trying to make things simpler. Thank you, *signora*. I'll be in touch. Right. Goodbye."

"What's she done that made life simpler?" Bree asked.

Gianni wanted to tell her but he had something else to tell her first.

"Later, *cara*."

"Now, Gianni. She said something that made you look like the cat that ate the canary."

"She did, but I want it to be a surprise." A surprise worthy of champagne and caviar. "Bree? Are you sure you don't want to go out for dinner?"

Didn't he want to spend their last evening alone in the house that almost felt like home?

"If you want to go out," she said stiffly, "we can."

"No. Staying home is fine. Staying in, that is. I mean, this isn't really our home. Our house. I mean—"

"I know what you mean," she said, and turned away from him.

He looked at her rigid back. He wanted to go to her and take her in his arms, tell her he was nervous as hell because he was going to ask her to stay married to him, that the *signora* had given him news that would be icing on the cake, but it was better to wait. Just a little longer. The baby would be asleep, they'd be alone…

Gianni cleared his throat and lifted Lucia from her baby

seat. "I'll put the baby to bed. You pour us some wine, okay?"

"Okay."

Bree waited until he'd left the kitchen. Then she sank down at the counter because she really wasn't sure her legs would hold her anymore.

She was a wreck. It was now or never time.

Somewhere between waking in Gianni's arms this morning and bathing Lucia this evening, she'd made a huge decision. She'd decided to tell him how she felt.

Well, not all of it. She'd say she was willing to stay married a little longer, if he wanted. If he said yes, that was exactly what he wanted, if his smile was loving, if he kissed her as tenderly as he had when he'd woken her in *Signora* Massini's blue bedroom, maybe she'd screw up the rest of her courage and admit she'd fallen in love with him.

But something had just happened. That call from the *signora*... What was that all about? A surprise, Gianni said, but only children believed that all surprises were good.

Should she change her plans?

No. No, she wouldn't. She was a gambler's daughter and for the first time in her life, she felt like gambling. Nothing ventured, nothing gained. Wasn't that what people said?

Briana took a deep breath and began taking things out of the refrigerator. A perfect dinner, an excellent wine and then—

And then, she'd do it.

NOTHING VENTURED, nothing gained...and nothing according to plan.

She set the table on the terrace. Halfway through their proscuitto and melon, a black cloud appeared from out of nowhere, stalled directly above them and drenched the terrace in rain.

Bree shrieked. Gianni laughed. They grabbed the wine,

the plates, the silverware and ran inside. At least the sudden downpour broke the silence that had settled over them.

"Are you soaked, *cara?* Do you want to change?"

Change? And delay things even more? "I'm fine."

"Good. I'll set the dining room table."

Bree brought in the chicken and mushrooms she'd made a hundred times before. Her "company for dinner" dish had never failed but it had, tonight. The chicken was rubbery, the mushrooms were soggy, and the winey sauce she'd spooned over the pasta tasted like burned vinegar.

"It's delicious," Gianni said bravely.

"It's awful," Bree said, and put down her fork. Nothing was going right. Talk about portents... "Gianni," she said, and at that same moment he said, "Briana."

Their eyes met. He put his fork on his plate and balled his hands into fists on the white linen table cloth, that muscle ticking in his jaw.

Bree's heart fell. He looked like a man about to have a root canal.

"You first," she said.

"No. You go ahead."

"I'd rather wait for you."

He nodded. He cleared his throat. He pushed back his chair, started to get to his feet, changed his mind and sat back again, hands still knotted, that little muscle ticking away like a metronome.

"Damn," he muttered. "Briana."

"Yes?"

"I have—I have something I've wanted to tell you for days."

Tic, tic, tic. "Go on."

"Let me tell you about *Signora* Massini's call first." That was the simpler part of what he wanted to tell her. Go for the easy stuff first. "It seems she's been thinking about Lucia's future. She's offered to sign papers that will eliminate the possibility of her making any future attempts to claim Lucia.''

It was wonderful news, but not what Bree had been hoping to hear.

''She also pointed out that our thirty days are up.'' He gave a strained smile. ''I assured her we were aware of that.''

Another little slide of the heart. Bree nodded. She didn't trust her voice.

''Her offer simplifies things considerably.'' He paused. ''It means Lucia can really be ours.''

''I don't understand. She *is* ours.''

''Well, yes.'' He hesitated. ''But there could have been difficulties because of our divorce.''

There was no place left for Bree's heart to slide, now that it was at her feet.

''Our divorce,'' she repeated.

''Exactly.'' Gianni leaned toward her and took her hand. ''I wasn't sure how a court would rule if we had to petition for Lucia's custody after we dissolved our marriage.''

''Dissolved our marriage,'' she said, like a well-trained parrot.

Gianni swallowed hard. This wasn't going well. Talking to a jury was turning out to be easier than baring your heart to the woman you loved. And why was she looking at him like that? He couldn't tell if she was angry or sad or happy and God, he wanted her to be happy.

''All I could come up with was that we'd have to stay married a little longer, and that wasn't what we'd agreed to do.''

''No,'' Bree said calmly, ''it wasn't.''

''Now the question is moot. The *signora's* not going to stand in our way.'' Gianni took a breath. Ready or not, it was truth time. ''No legal battles ahead, *cara*. No need for me to ask you to prolong our arrangement. We can go home and simply be together.''

"Sleep together, you mean.''

Gianni looked blank. ''Well, of course. But—''

"No.''

"Excuse me?''

She pulled her hand from his. ''I said, we're not going to go home to this—this happy little fiction you've created.''

"Briana, listen to me—''

"I did listen.'' Bree shoved back her chair and rose to her feet. ''You're right. The good news is that we won't have to prolong our arrangement.''

"No. We won't, *cara,* because—''

"Do not call me that again!''

Gianni shot to his feet. What in hell was happening? He'd told his wife that Lucia could be theirs, that they could adopt her and be her real parents. Now, he'd told her he didn't want a divorce. And she was looking at him as if she wanted to kill him.

"What's wrong with you?'' He could feel his temper rising and he fought to keep it under control. ''Don't you want Lucia? Don't you want to be with me?''

"I want Lucia. I do *not* want to 'be' with you.''

His eyes narrowed. ''But I thought—all these weeks, the times we made love—''

"I know what you thought. Our arrangement would end. Sleeping together wouldn't.''

"Will you forget the damned arrangement?''

"Stop shouting.''

"I am not shouting,'' he yelled, and slammed his fist on the table. ''I'm talking sense, which is more than you're doing.''

"I am talking sense, *signore.* You just don't like what I'm saying.''

"What the hell are you so angry about?''

"The fact that you can ask me that means there's no point trying to explain it to you."

Gianni laughed wildly, stabbed his hands into his hair and looked up.

"She's crazy," he told the ceiling. "Absolutely insane!"

"You mean, I *was* crazy. I'm perfectly sane now."

"Damn it to hell," he roared.

Lucia began to wail.

"Now see what you've done," Bree said. "You woke the baby."

"Bree." Gianni took a deep breath. She didn't want to stay married to him. She didn't love him. No. He couldn't, he wouldn't believe it. "Briana," he said carefully, "we have to talk."

"We just did. It's over."

"Damn it to hell, Bree…"

"You already said that."

"Briana," he said, his voice rough with warning, "I forbid you to do this!"

Bree laughed. Laughed, damn it!

"You never did get it, Firelli," she said. "I don't take orders."

She strode past him and while he was still trying to decide what in hell had just happened, he heard the nursery door slam shut and the lock click home.

CHAPTER THIRTEEN

GIANNI DIDN'T even come after her.

Bree heard the front door slam, then the roar of the Ferrari as he tore down the driveway.

Good. Fine. If she moved quickly enough, she'd never have to see him again until after the divorce, and then only when it involved Lucia.

The baby was still sobbing. Bree lifted her from the crib and cradled her against her breast.

"Don't cry, sweetheart," she crooned. "Everything's going to be fine."

The baby's sobs became whimpers. Bree kissed her forehead, held her a little longer, then lay her gently in the crib.

"You and I are going on a trip," she whispered. "Won't that be fun?"

Lucia gave a last, ragged sob before her lashes drooped to her plump cheeks. Bree bent over the crib and kissed her. Then she made her way to the master suite.

The suite she'd shared with Gianni.

The rumpled bed where Gianni had carried her, lazy as a cat from an afternoon spent in the sun, seemed to take up half a wall.

"You need a nap, *cara,*" he'd said, but what he'd done to her on the silky sheets had nothing to do with napping. He'd kissed her, touched her, brought her to climax after climax...

The calculating, self-serving, autocratic son of a bitch!

She'd *never* loved him. Not for a moment. It had been

lust. Her brothers called it Zipper-Think Syndrome and believed it was their own private joke.

Bree pulled open the closet door.

Wrong. She'd known about their guys-are-all-the-same comedy routine for years. The only surprise was finding out the hard way that being led around by your hormones wasn't something that only happened to men.

She swung her suitcase onto the bed, yanked open a dresser drawer so hard it almost fell to the floor.

Fallon had accused her of never having experienced real passion. Well, she thought grimly, she had now—and to hell with it. And as if that weren't bad enough, she'd turned out to be such a damned goody-goody that she'd had to kid herself into thinking what she'd felt for Gianni was love.

How could she have been so stupid?

Love was a lie perpetuated on women by men determined to turn them into androids.

Bree tossed her clothes into the suitcase. Not everything. She'd brought only enough for a weekend and when Gianni the Emperor decided they'd have to stay longer, he'd taken the baby and her on a whirlwind shopping trip. She'd bought half a dozen things for herself but the next day, the store had delivered boxes filled with virtually everything she'd tried on or even looked at.

"I didn't buy these things," she'd said.

The emperor had smiled. "I did, *cara*. It was my pleasure."

Damned right, his pleasure. This entire month had been about him and his pleasure. For all she knew, he'd hatched this thirty day scheme for his pleasure.

"You can take these things and stuff them," Bree told the room as she marched back and forth between the closet, the dresser and her suitcase. "I don't want them any more than I want you."

A shrink would probably tell her that her reactions were

understandable. She'd lived a lifetime in a month. Karen's death, the news about the baby, Gianni shouldering his way into her world and dragging her off to a place time had forgotten, all of it capped by a phony marriage...

At least one good thing had come out of it.

Lucia.

Bree sank down on the edge of the bed. All those years, drifting from job to job and place to place, searching for something without knowing what she'd been searching for and now here it was, sweetly wrapped in pink.

Who'd have believed she'd find so much joy in being Mom to this little girl? She wasn't; not really. She knew that, but for a while it had seemed as if she was.

They'd been a family. She, the baby, Gianni.

Tears stung her eyes, though she couldn't imagine why. She'd always known her arrangement with Gianni wasn't going to be permanent, and if she'd clung to the desperate hope he'd want to change that, whose fault was it but her own?

What she felt for Lucia was the only kind of love that had meaning.

Bree drew a shuddering breath. What now? A minute ago, she'd been filled with energy. Now, she wanted only to curl into a ball and sleep. No. She wouldn't do that. The thought of sleeping under the same roof as Gianni tonight made her shudder. Getting on the plane with him tomorrow, following docilely as he took her to the apartment he'd decided she and Lucia would share, would be even worse.

She wasn't his property. He couldn't tell her what to do...

And she didn't have to live next door and watch him go on with his life as if this month had never happened.

What she'd told him was true. They didn't have to live side by side. They didn't even have to live in the same state. Divorced couples—those who'd really been married— shared custody of children with one parent on one coast, one on the other. Why should sharing guardianship be any different?

Why hadn't she thought of that right away?

Bree hissed a word that hadn't passed her lips since the days her brothers used to waylay their sisters and dump them, fully dressed, into the pool at the Desert Song.

It was time to reclaim her life.

Okay. She needed a plan, and fast. Getting out of here before Gianni returned was number one. She knew she'd never be able to control her temper, and she didn't want to give him anything, not even a show of fury.

He wasn't worth it.

Leaving was easy enough. Pack some stuff for the baby— she damned well wasn't leaving Lucia behind—call a taxi, tell the cabbie to take her…

Where?

The easy choice was her sister's home on the other side of this same island. She'd made a point of not getting in touch with Fallon. How could she have explained a marriage that wasn't a marriage? She could do it now, she supposed…

No. That wouldn't work. The last place to escape Gianni was in the home of his best friend.

Bree chewed on her lip.

She could go back to New York, hole up in her apartment…and find Gianni on her doorstep, demanding compliance with the plan he'd laid out for her life.

Boston, then. To Cullen. Forget that. Cullen and his wife had a brand new baby. So did Keir and Cassie. Sean was still on his honeymoon, and Megan was off on a diplomatic trip with her husband.

Too bad. Meg, of all of them, would have understood. She'd also married for expediency. But it wasn't the same at all. It turned out that Meg and Qasim had loved each other from the beginning. It had just taken them a while to acknowledge it.

Gianni had never loved her. Never. And she—she—

Bree swallowed hard. She had never loved him, either.

She needed a safe harbor. A place where nobody would hand her over to Gianni before she was ready to deal with him. Once they were divorced, she'd meet with him and work out details as they concerned Lucia.

There was only one place to go. Las Vegas. Vegas was the capital of quick marriages and almost-as-quick divorces. It was also her home, at least, it had been for most of her life.

There was only one drawback. Its name was Mary Elizabeth O'Connell-Coyle. Facing her mother, explaining the situation, wouldn't be fun, but one look at Lucia and Mary Elizabeth would melt.

And keeping Gianni away would be easy. All she'd have to do was tell her stepfather she didn't want Gianni to come near her and that would be that.

Just let *Signore* Firelli try and blow past the Desert Song's security team.

Decision made, Bree moved quickly. Her suitcase was packed. Now, she filled a diaper bag with stuff for the baby, phoned the airport and called for a taxi. The only thing left to do was write a note for Gianni. For all she knew, he'd be just as happy to come back and find her gone but he'd surely worry about Lucia.

Bree grabbed a pen and a piece of paper.

Lucia is with me, she scrawled. *I'll contact you as soon as I've finalized my plans.*

She read the note aloud. Good. It was direct and definite, the way she should have been from the start. She propped the note on a table in the hall, just as a car pulled up in the driveway. Her heart leaped. Was it Gianni? Had he come back to tell her—to tell her—

A horn beeped. Bree let out a breath she didn't know she'd been holding. It was the cab; no Ferrari would ever make such a pathetic sound.

She opened the door. *"Uno momento,"* she yelled.

Then she scooped up the baby and everything else, and closed the door on what surely had been four weeks of madness.

BREE PHONED her mother from the airport.

"Hi," she said brightly. "You guys in the mood for a visit?"

"Oh, sweetheart, that would be lovely. When?"

Bree hesitated. "How about right now?"

"You mean, you're here? In Las Vegas?"

"Yes. Is that okay? If you and Dan are busy..."

"Briana, what a thing to say. We'd love to see you. This is a wonderful surprise."

"Actually—actually, I have another surprise, Ma." Bree hesitated. She wanted to be careful with this. Her mother had recovered from a stroke only a few months ago. A surprise, even one that was smiling and making tiny bubbles through a rosebud mouth, might need delicate handling. "I, ah, I have someone with me."

As soon as she'd spoken, she knew she'd phrased it badly. She could almost see Mary happily leaping to the wrong conclusion.

"I'm delighted to hear it! What's his name?"

Here we go, Bree thought, and took a steadying breath. "It's not a 'he,' Mother, it's a baby."

There was an almost endless pause. "Excuse me?"

Bree closed her eyes. She was exhausted—she'd had to change planes twice—and hungry and depressed, though she couldn't figure out why. She'd survived the Month From Hell. What was there to be depressed about?

"A baby," she said wearily. "Ma? It's probably easier if I explain everything when I see you."

"Just tell me one thing, Bree. Is this child yours?"

"Yes. No." Bree sighed. "She's mine, legally. Did I give birth to her? No."

"Ah. In that case," Mary said, sounding a little disappointed, "I suppose there really isn't a man in your life."

"Not anymore," Bree said, and hung up the phone.

THEY WERE WAITING for her at the hotel entrance. Her mother, looking healthy and beautiful; her stepfather, his face creased in a puzzled but welcoming smile. Mary hugged Bree, looked at Lucia, and sighed with delight.

"Oh my, aren't you precious? What's your name, sweetie?"

"Her name is Lucia. Do you remember my friend, Karen? She came here with me for spring break our second year in college?"

"Yes, of course."

"Karen and her husband were in a terrible accident. They—they didn't survive it. It turned out they'd named me Lucia's guardian."

Amazing, how easily the story could be told, if she just left out the part about Gianni. That could come later.

Mary's smile softened. "How sad," she said gently. Her eyes met Briana's. "Karen made a good choice, naming you to care for her daughter."

Bree blinked. She'd always assumed her mother saw her as a gypsy. "Do you think so?"

"Of course, darling. You have the biggest heart in the world." Smiling again, Mary held out her arms. "Hello, Lucy. You come right here, to Grandma."

"But she's not—"

She's not actually my daughter, Bree started to say, but

the truth was, Lucia—Lucy, as Mary had already dubbed her—was her child, in her heart.

Gianni treated her as if she were his child, too. If only she and Gianni…if only their marriage…

"Bree?" Mary's smile faded. She handed the baby to Dan and moved toward Briana. "Darling girl, what's the matter?"

Bree shook her head. She'd never been much for unloading her troubles on Mary. Her mother had always been busy juggling enough problems of her own.

"Sweetheart," Mary said softly, "please, what is it? You look as if your heart is breaking."

A cry burst from Briana's throat. "It is," she sobbed, and flew into her mother's arms.

BREE SAT on a high-backed stool at the kitchen counter, hands wrapped around a mug of tea.

Mary had been wonderful. No questions, no lectures. She'd simply herded them all up to the penthouse, tucked Lucia into a crib magically produced by Housekeeping, sent Dan off on an errand, then put the tea to brew.

"Herbal," she said, "to relax you."

Now she was bustling about the kitchen. Mary had a housekeeper and cook; she'd had people to "do" for her for years but that never kept her from doing lots of things herself.

"But why, Ma?" Bree remembered asking once, when her mother was hurrying to get dinner on the table.

"Because it makes me happy," Mary had replied.

Because it's what Pa expects, Bree had thought. Watching her mother now, she wondered if she'd been wrong. Ruarch was long gone, but her mother still loved to fuss. She'd made the tea and cinnamon toast because she knew it had been one of Briana's childhood favorites. Now she was peeling potatoes, then carrots, pausing to check on whatever it was in the oven that smelled so heavenly.

"Roast beef," Mary said, and Bree realized she'd asked about it out loud. "It's Dan's favorite."

Bree took a sip of tea. "Pa's was meatloaf."

Mary smiled. "You remember that, hmm?"

"How could I forget? You made it once a week."

"Well, of course. I made it because your father loved it, the same as I made chocolate chip cookies for you, vanilla pudding for Sean... It's a joy, doing things for people you love."

Bree put down her mug. "Is that the reason you never said anything whenever Pa uprooted you and dragged you off to some new place?"

She hadn't expected to ask the question. Now that she had, though, she was glad it was out. Her mother's hands stilled for a second. Then she smiled and went on working.

"He didn't drag me, Briana. Where did you get that idea?"

"Oh, I could tell. You'd get that look on your face. That 'not again' look."

"Not again?" Mary shook her head. "If that's what you thought, you were wrong. I admit, it wasn't easy, starting over each time." She wiped her hands on a towel, poured herself some tea and smiled across the counter at Briana. "But I understood that your father needed to keep searching for his dream."

"I see."

"No," Mary said gently, "you don't. Go on, Bree. Say what's on your mind."

Bree looked up. The question, so long unasked, came easily to her lips. "What about your dream, Ma? Didn't that count for anything?"

"Your father was my dream, Briana. And before you tell

me what you've longed to tell me for years, that I let him run my life—''

''I never said—''

''You didn't have to, darling. You were as transparent as glass.'' Mary reached for her daughter's hand. ''He was my dream, and I was his.''

''I'm not saying he didn't love you.''

''You'd better not,'' Mary said, smiling, but with a steel undertone in her voice. ''Your father was a gambler. So was I. I gave up a staid, stultifying life for one that was unpredictable and always exciting. I followed the man I loved.'' She leaned closer. ''Your father would come home and say, 'Mary, darlin', I've heard of a wondrous new opportunity.' And I'd say, 'You tell me about it, Ruarch, while I start packing.' If you think that's a weakness, Briana, to love someone enough to be willing to walk beside him no matter where the path leads, then you've yet to fall in love. Truly, passionately in love.''

Fallon had told her the same thing weeks ago. Were her mother and sister right? Had she seen her passion for Gianni as a weakness?

What she'd felt for him had terrified her.

''Bree? Honey, you *have* fallen in love, haven't you? I can see it in your eyes.''

Tears suddenly streaked Briana's face. ''It's too late,'' she said in a broken whisper. ''Besides, it doesn't matter. He was my dream, but I wasn't his.''

''Oh, sweetheart.'' Mary dug in her pocket and took out a tissue. ''Dry your eyes, blow your nose, and tell me everything.''

Bree started at the beginning and left nothing out, spared herself nothing, not even how much she loved Gianni. How she longed for him to return that love, to adore her as she adored him, to cherish as real the vows they'd taken at their wedding.

"I want to be with him for the rest of my life, but he doesn't want that." She looked at her mother, her eyes still wet with tears but shining with defiance. "I won't be someone he can discard when he tires of me."

"Are you certain that's how he feels, Briana? Have you talked to him?"

"He told me," Bree said, her voice breaking. "He said we didn't have to worry about legal battles with Lucia's great-grandmother anymore. He said our marriage—our make-believe marriage—wasn't a problem. He wants the divorce we agreed upon the day we married." She swallowed dryly. "And I'm going to give it to him. Then I'll move a million miles away, far enough so I never have to see him again except where it concerns Lucia, and—"

"And exactly how do you propose to do all that," a furious male voice demanded, "when I will not permit it?"

Briana's eyes widened. Her mother looked past her, the expression on her face changing from concern to curiosity.

"Answer me, Briana. How will you divorce me without my permission?"

Bree stood up, took a long breath and turned around. Gianni stood in the breakfast room, arms folded, legs apart, his face drawn into a scowl. He was a study in rage.

Her heart—her foolish, foolish heart—rose. Then she remembered that he was a man who wanted to control a woman. Who wanted her body, not her love. And she knew she would not, must not, let him see how much he had hurt her.

Bree lifted her chin. "What are you doing here, Gianni? I told you I'd contact you."

"Once your plans were final," he said coldly. "Yes. I found that a particularly charming line for a wife to leave in a note to her husband."

"I am your wife only for the moment."

"You are my wife for as long as I say you are." Gianni's

gaze shifted to Mary Elizabeth. "You must be my wife's mother."

"For the last time, Firelli, I am not your—"

"I am," Mary said politely, holding out her hand. "How, um, nice to meet you, Mister Firelli." She shot a look at Bree. "My daughter's told me a great deal about you."

Gianni grinned. "Lies, all of it," he said, taking Mary's hand and bringing it to his lips. "I'm delighted to meet you, Mrs. Coyle, despite the circumstances."

"Mary, please."

"What is this?" Bree said hotly. "My mother's happy to meet you, you're happy to meet her? And how'd you get up here, anyway? Security doesn't let anyone on this floor without permission."

His smile fled, as did his charm. "We can discuss that later. For now, get your things. And the baby. You're coming with me."

"She's not going anywhere she doesn't want to go," Dan said, stepping out from behind Gianni. "Bree. Honey, this man says he's your husband." His eyes narrowed on Gianni. "But I'll throw him out myself, if that's what you want."

"Don't try it," Gianni said softly. "You're Briana's stepfather and I'd like to start on the right footing but this is between my wife and me."

"Stop saying that," Bree snapped. "I am *not* your wife."

"I have a marriage certificate that says you are."

"It's a piece of paper."

"An official piece of paper. Get your things, Briana. I'm tired, I'm hungry, I'm mad as hell and I refuse to waste time discussing something that's already been decided."

Bree stared at him. He *was* tired; there were dark shadows under his eyes and stubble on his determined jaw. She wanted to go to him and kiss the shadows away.

Was she crazy? Who gave a damn if he had shadows under his eyes? He could have craters, for all she cared.

And why was she thinking of him as her husband? He wouldn't be, not in a couple of weeks.

"There's nothing to discuss."

Gianni looked at his watch. "I'll give you five minutes. Then I'm taking Lucia under one arm, you under the other, and leaving."

"Oh, please! That Sicilian routine won't work here."

He took a step toward her, his eyes hot on hers. "Did you really think you could run away from me, *cara?* Did you think I wouldn't come after you?"

"Don't *'cara'* me, either. What's the matter, *signore?* Did I dent your ego? Is it always you who does the leaving?"

"What the hell are you talking about?"

"Give me a break, Firelli. You know damned well what I'm talking about. You're the man. You do the leaving, not me."

Gianni folded his arms. He had to do something with them, otherwise he knew he'd reach for Briana, grab her by the shoulders, shake her until she admitted she loved him and wanted him because, damn it, she *had* to feel the way he felt or he'd go crazy.

"You can't leave me," he said smugly. "You can't divorce me, not without my approval."

"Welcome to the real world, *signore.*" Bree folded her arms, too, in unconscious imitation. "This is the good old U.S. of A., not *la Sicilia.* I can and will divorce you, and you can't stop me."

"But I can, *cara,*" he said softly, a thin smile curving his lips. "Our marriage was performed in Italy."

"So?"

"So," he said, the lie as sweet and simple as sugar on his tongue, "it can only be dissolved there."

Bree jerked back. "What?"

"I said—"

"I heard what you said. I don't believe you. You were the one who said I could go to Mexico or the Caribbean for a divorce, remember?"

He remembered, all right. What a stupid thing to have told her, but he'd said it before he'd been willing to admit he was head over heels in love with this stubborn, impossible, headstrong, magnificent woman.

"I was wrong."

"Ha! The great emperor, wrong?" Bree tossed her head. "Impossible."

"There won't be a divorce, *cara*," he said softly. "You and our baby are coming home with me."

Our baby. The words were so right. If only he meant them.

"No," Bree said, and hated herself for the little tremor in her voice. "I'm not going with you, Gianni. I don't want to live the way you've planned." She felt the sting of tears again. *God,* she thought, *God, please, don't let me cry.* "I know you'll be a good guardian for Lucia. I didn't mean it when I said I'd move a million miles away, but I won't live next door to you. I won't sleep with you—"

"You won't live next door," Gianni said softly, "you'll live with me, and you'll sleep with me, make love with me, because you're my wife, my heart, and I'm not giving you up, Briana. Not ever."

Silence filled the kitchen. Then Mary cleared her throat. "Dan? Now might be the perfect time for me to show you that area in the casino that needs re-decorating."

"Now?" Dan said incredulously. "Right now?"

"Right now," Mary said firmly, slipping past Briana, pausing just long enough to kiss her cheek and whisper something in her ear. "Good luck, Mr. Firelli," she said softly.

"It's Gianni," he said, his eyes never leaving Bree's.

Mary smiled. "Indeed. Relatives should never stand on formality."

"Relatives?" Briana said. "Relatives? Mother, for heaven's sake…"

She was talking to the air. Her mother had taken her stepfather's arm and tugged him from the room. In the distance, a door slammed.

Briana and Gianni were alone.

Gianni came closer. Bree stepped back but there was no place to go; the counter was behind her. Her husband was in front of her. But he wasn't her husband. He didn't want to be her husband.

"You can't divorce me, *cara,*" he said softly.

"Of course I can." Bree meant to sound determined; instead, she sounded heartbroken. She couldn't let him see that she was weak. She couldn't! "That was our arrangement, remember?"

His gaze was like a caress on her lips. "I remember everything," he whispered, framing her face with his hands. "Everything," he said, and brushed his mouth over hers.

"Gianni. Don't."

"Why not? You're mine. If I want to kiss you, I can."

"I am *not* yours. I'm not anyone's. I'm—"

"You're right. You belong to yourself, Briana—and I love you all the more for it."

He drew her to him. She was stiff. Unyielding, but as his arms closed around her, a little sigh whispered from her lips.

"Cara." He put his hand under her chin. "Look at me. Yes. Like that. With your heart, your soul in your eyes." Gianni smiled. "You said you wanted a divorce and I believed you, but I was a fool. A woman who trembles in a man's arms, who gives everything she is to him, is not a woman who wants to leave a man."

"No! I don't know why you'd think—"

He brushed his lips over hers again, his mouth lingering,

warm and sweet against hers. Bree fought against it but it happened anyway, her lips softening, clinging to his, her hands lifting to his chest.

"I love you, Bree. And you love me."

"No! I don't love you, Gianni. I don't know why you'd think—"

He kissed her again and she trembled. "You always talked about complications, but nothing could have been more complicated than what happened the night I finally worked up enough courage to tell you I wanted us to have a real marriage."

"What?"

"I made a mess of it, Bree. It took me hours to realize how badly I'd screwed up." He framed her face with his hands. "I wanted to make it perfect, *cara*. Telling you how much I loved you. Telling you that the *signora* had agreed to let us adopt our little girl—"

Bree's eyes widened. "Oh, Gianni," she whispered. "Did she really say that?"

He nodded. "And you told me that you couldn't wait to leave me."

"No. Oh, no. I never said—"

"You didn't, *cara*. I realized it after I calmed down." Gianni drew her close and kissed her again, a long, tender kiss that threatened to melt her bones. "You misunderstood me, and your pride made you answer the only way you could." Smiling, he ran his thumb over her bottom lip. "You were wonderful. Tough. Brave... But you damned near broke my heart."

Briana looped her arms around her husband's neck.

"I thought loving you was a weakness," she said softly. "But I was wrong. Loving you is my strength, Gianni. It's what I was meant for. It's—"

"Everything *cara*. I know, because it's like that for me, too."

They smiled into each other's eyes, a man and woman who'd spent their lives looking for each other. Then the soft sounds of a baby waking up drifted into the room.

"Lucia?" Gianni said.

"My mother calls her Lucy."

Gianni grinned. "Sounds like a good American name to me."

One more sweet, deep kiss. Then Gianni slipped his arm around his wife and they went to claim their daughter.

DOWNSTAIRS, in his office, Dan Coyle looked at his wife and tried to figure out what was going on.

"I don't follow any of this, Duchess," he said. "Our Bree comes home with a child that isn't hers, tells you she's married to a man she wants to divorce, he turns up and you abandon her?" He shook his head. "It's beyond me to understand, but I suppose you know what you're doing."

Mary Elizabeth O'Connell-Coyle patted her husband's hand.

"What I'm doing, my love, is planning a wedding. I'm sure Briana and Gianni will want a real one, now that everything's settled."

"What's settled?" Dan asked in bewilderment.

"Why, everything," Mary replied gently. "We have each other, and all six of my children are happily wed. What more could a woman ask?"

Dan smiled, leaned in and kissed her.

"What more could anyone ask," he said softly, "than to find love?"

HARLEQUIN®
Presents

Seduction and Passion Guaranteed!

Legally wed, but he's never said…
"I love you."

They're…

Wedlocked!

The series
in which
marriages are
made in haste…
and love
comes later…

**Look out for more Wedlocked! marriage stories
in Harlequin Presents throughout 2005.**

Coming in May:
THE DISOBEDIENT BRIDE
by Helen Bianchin
#2463

Coming in June:
THE MORETTI MARRIAGE
by Catherine Spencer
#2474

HARLEQUIN®
Presents

Seduction and Passion Guaranteed!

Introducing a brand-new trilogy by

Sharon Kendrick

THE ROYAL HOUSE OF CACCIATORE

Passion, power & privilege – the dynasty continues
with these handsome princes...

Welcome to Mardivino—a beautiful and wealthy
Mediterranean island principality, with a prestigious
and glamorous royal family. There are three
Cacciatore princes—Nicolo, Guido and
the eldest, the heir, Gianferro.

Next month (May 05), meet Nico in
THE MEDITERRANEAN
PRINCE'S PASSION #2466

Coming in June: Guido's story, in
THE PRINCE'S LOVE-CHILD #2472

Coming soon: Gianferro's story in
THE FUTURE KING'S BRIDE

Only from Harlequin Presents